HANGMAN'S ROW

By Aaron Marc Stein

HANGMAN'S ROW

AARON MARC STEIN

PUBLISHED FOR THE CRIME CLUB BY
DOUBLEDAY & COMPANY, INC.
GARDEN CITY, NEW YORK
1982

All of the characters in this book
are fictitious, and any resemblance
to actual persons, living or dead,
is purely coincidental.

·

Library of Congress Cataloging in Publication Data

Stein, Aaron Marc, 1906–
Hangman's row.

I. Title.
PS3537.T3184H36   813'.52
AACR2
ISBN: 0-385-17945-6
Library of Congress Catalog Card Number 81-43397

To
the memory of
Jonathan Carroll

HANGMAN'S ROW

CHAPTER 1

I can't wish that girls were resistible. Life would be far less worth living if they were. It would be simpler, and it would carry much less hazard but, as the poet said in another connection, it would be flat, stale, and unprofitable. Similarly, I cannot wish that I might somehow develop an increased resistance to their allure. Being lured is too much fun, and anyhow it would be a futile wish. At the Mad Hatter's tea party Alice hit it on the nose: she couldn't have more tea when she hadn't had any. You can't increase something that isn't there in the first place. If there is one thing I can tell you about Matt Erridge with anything like certainty, it is that he is totally without resistance.

I am Matt Erridge. In other respects I'm a sensible, hardheaded sort of guy. Since I am an engineer, I know how to calculate stresses. So if I tell you that the stresses exerted on Erridge by feminine allure are incalculable, I should be believed.

There was a big job shaping up and a strong possibility that I was going to be tapped for it. Since a large part of the financing for it was to be Dutch money, for the preliminary discussions of projected costs, feasibility, and all such requisite boredom I had been asked to go where the money was. Such discussions have a way of stringing out. Each actual session may run to an hour or two. Intervals between sessions usually run to days.

So it's mostly waiting around, and a man finds ways to fill in the waiting time. In Amsterdam there's cheese, there's gin, there are herrings and canals. There's the Rijksmuseum for a look at Rembrandts and Vermeers, there's a whole museum full of Van Goghs, and there's always girl-watching.

Oddly enough, it happened that nothing could have been farther from my mind than girl-watching at that moment when I first saw the girl. I had wandered into the Van Gogh museum. Maybe you're aware of Vincent Van Gogh as that poor crazy who cut off his ear, but you only have to go into that museum to be convinced that cutting off his ear was far from being the most extraordinary thing the man did. Floor after floor, picture after picture, it's one dazzler after another. After looking at only a few of them you begin to feel that you have been beaten into submission. You go on in something like a stupor.

Then in the middle of everything there was this one landscape that stopped me cold. It was as though I had been handed a new pair of eyes. People kept streaming past me, methodically moving along from one canvas to the next, but I was frozen. That one landscape was giving me lessons in how to see. Trees and grass, fields and fences, sunlight and shade from there on out were going to have a different look for me.

I later realized that I hadn't even heard her when she first spoke.

"Below the belt."

Those were the first of her words that came through to me. Since they did come through, I turned to look at her. She was standing beside me and she was looking at the painting. She was young and she looked like something out of an old movie. You may not have been around back when Ginger Rogers was doing them, but you're likely to have seen them in little chopped-up chunks between TV commercials. It was the ugly-duckling gimmick where wrong clothes, wrong hairdo, and wrong everything were supposed to suck you away from noticing that here was a nymph just about to grow up into being a goddess. Before the movie was over, of course, there was always the transformation.

I doubt that those beginnings ever fooled anyone. I know they never fooled me, and at my first sight of this girl in the museum I wasn't fooled either. Her hair was brown and short and it looked as though each strand had a mind of its own. They weren't long enough to be tangled, but they were going every which way. She was wearing what are known as sensible shoes, and hers were so uncompromisingly sensible that they were guaranteed to offend any man's sensibilities. Her blue jeans contributed nothing, since those areas for which jeans can do much were hidden from view. From neck to knee she was shrouded in a sweater. It was one of those heavy jobs that is more like a collision mat than a garment, and it would have been big on a kid three times her weight. The sought-after effect might have been unisex, but it wasn't. It was simply inanimate. It could only have been some sixth sense that was telling me that under that monstrous encasement of knit and purl there lurked all the right little curvaceous forms in all the right places. Certainly nothing showed.

"Below the belt?" I repeated after her.

"I said you looked as though you had just been hit below the belt," she said.

"Stupid?"

"Stupefied. Thunderstruck. Knocked all of a heap."

"Aren't *you?*" I asked.

"Every time I see it," she said. "I thought that with time the effect might wear off, but now I think it never will. There's just no getting used to it."

"You come here often?" I asked.

"All the time. It's what I do."

"Have you seen all of them?"

"Repeatedly," she said. "I'm writing a paper on him."

"Should I be looking at the rest of them?"

"If you want to."

"I don't want to. This one's mine."

"When he painted it, he thought it might be the best thing he'd ever done."

"Puts me in good company, doesn't it?"

"Van Gogh and you," she said. "Not bad."

"And you."

"Yes," she said, "and me."

"A paper," I said. "School?"

"For my Master's."

"Infant prodigy," I said.

"That's condescending."

"It isn't," I said. "It's more like envious."

"You're not all that old."

"Nor that young. Can I ask you a question without your getting mad?"

"If it's that kind of a question, can I answer it without your getting mad?"

"I'm convinced," I said. "You're not as young as you look."

"That's not a question."

"No," I said, "just a digression. You have taste. Beauty knocks you out."

"Obviously. Otherwise I'd be doing economics or sociology or something."

"Right. So why do you dress the way you do?"

"Because I come here to look and not to be looked at."

"That's ungenerous. Would being looked at interfere with your looking?"

"You just don't know," she said. "I grant you that here it's not as bad as it is in Italy. Up here men don't whack, but still . . ."

"So that's why you wear the collision mat?"

"The what?"

"Collision mat."

"What's a collision mat?"

I did my best to explain it, but it wasn't much good. She had never traveled by ship. She belonged to the airborne generation. I suggested that we move it to a little bar alongside the nearest canal.

There would be something moving on the canal even if it was only a sightseeing boat. I could show her a collision mat. I could have told her that it was the thing they put out to protect a boat's paintwork from scraping against a pier, but I couldn't see where that would lead to anything.

She came out to a bar with me, and I had a half hour while I worked on some beer and she worked on some tea. I did get to show her a few collision mats, but it stopped right there. She wouldn't let me see her home. She turned down my suggestion of dinner that evening. She was adamant in her rejection of any suggestion that I might see her again.

"Why not?" I said. "If I may quote you, you did say I'm 'not all that old.'"

"That's the trouble."

"What's the trouble?"

"You're not old enough. If you were an old man . . ." She left it hanging.

"I'm aging with every minute," I said.

"It would be that I picked you up."

"And didn't you?"

"Yes, but only to share the landscape. It was nice sharing it with someone who could see."

"It was very nice," I said. "Surely that's an indication that there could be other things for us to share."

"If you had picked me up, it might have been different."

"Then let's start over again," I suggested. "I'm Matt Erridge and I want to know a lot more about Van Gogh. You know all about him, and you are . . . ?"

"Too late," she said. "Starting over would be no more than role playing. The fact would remain that I picked you up, and that's something I don't do."

She even wanted to pay for her cup of tea, but I wouldn't have any of that. Behaving as though she were giving me some great break, she permitted me to win that one small point. She thanked me prettily for the tea and she took off. I very much wanted to follow her, but the image of an old goat forcing his attentions on a little girl kept me where I was. I compensated myself with a gin and with the thought that there would always be other girls and with the resolution to remember thereafter that I had to be the one to make the first move.

I did go back to the museum, hitting it at the same hour the next day, but she wasn't there. I was left with telling myself that I would have gotten nowhere even if she had been there.

The whole nature of girl-watching had, of course, changed. It was no longer taking simple enjoyment in whatever happened to come by. Now it was focused. I was watching for her. Amsterdam is no small town. It's a big city and it swarms with people. You might be thinking that there wasn't much chance of my happening on her again, but I was full of hope. Amsterdam has its museum district, three big ones in a great clump. That district, furthermore, is a pleasant part of town. There were worse places a man could choose for doing his hanging out.

I did see her again and, against all expectations, it was at a time when I wasn't even looking. It was the evening of the next day and museums aren't open in late evenings. Even a girl who is doing a paper on Van Gogh isn't likely to be frequenting those parts after closing time. I was walking back to my hotel after dinner. It had been a business dinner, starchily formal.

My host had been Jan Van Mieris, the big-money man, and he lived in a big-money house. It was an old one, a seventeenth-century merchant's house, high and handsome on the flower-encrusted bank of the city's most beautiful canal. Van Mieris was also an art collector, and his Mondriaans and Van Goghs looked comfortably at home in the great old rooms. Skillfully steering the talk into the right openings, my host had managed to let it be known that an ancestor had built the house and that all his forebears that had come along since had been born behind its rosy brick walls and had also died there. He himself had been born in the house and he was looking forward to dying there. To die anywhere else would be spitting in the face of history.

It had been a good enough evening if not a merry one. I liked Jan Van Mieris, but there had been too much food, too much drink, too much aroma of Dutch cigar smoke, and too much talk of dying. When I pulled away at the correct hour—ten-thirty on the dot—I needed to walk off the food and the drink and, more than anything, I needed air.

It was a long walk. It took me through quiet streets, along peaceful canals, and across a succession of bridges. It was on one of the bridges that I saw her. I don't know that I wouldn't have gone by without taking any notice of her if it hadn't been for the collision mat. It was that stupendous hunk of sweater that caught my eye. I headed straight for it. I was determined that this time it would be Erridge who made the first move and spoke the first word.

I was moving in with the conviction that there couldn't be two such sweaters. As I drew up closer, however, I found myself beginning to believe the unbelievable. I could have sworn that it was the same sweater, but at the same time I was telling myself that it couldn't be. The way I was seeing it then, it appeared to be filled as she could never have filled it.

The occupant was sitting perched on the bridge rail and not alone. Even the collision mat couldn't conceal or disguise an impressive span of shoulders. The sleeves were pushed up above the elbows, and the exposed forearms were thick and hairy. It was a guy inside the thing and the muscular arms were wrapped around a girl. The arms were hairy, but the head was hairier—a great mop of blond curls and a comparable bush of golden beard.

Of the girl he had in his arms there wasn't much I could see. In that big guy's embrace she was all but surrounded. Since she was in the process of being kissed, her face was almost totally submerged in the golden underbrush. Not without some minor pangs of envy I stepped onto the bridge. I was just going to walk past and continue on my way. Erridge is no spoilsport. I am a firm believer in love and let love.

But I had no sooner set foot on the bridge than the girl pulled away. I saw her and she saw me and all my determination that another time I would be the first one to speak went down the drain. I'd like to think that it was tact that held me back, that some reflex of gentlemanliness was going to carry me past them without any indication that I had recognized her.

I can't be certain of that. It may well have been that I was just struck dumb with astonishment and too much buffeted by quick change. I had pegged the sweater and had thought we'd been about to meet. Then I had become aware of what was in the sweater and I had lost interest only to find immediately that we were meeting. Ping-Pong balls adjust to that kind of rapid back and forth, but it's more than can be expected of a man.

There was also the transformation. It used to be well into the movie before Ginger Rogers did the moth-out-of-the-chrysalis bit. She was again in a sweater, but now it was a sweater and skirt. It was also shoes that allowed her ankles to look like ankles. Her hair had had the guidance of a hairbrush. It now knew the way to go. I took the whole of it in, but it was the sweater that got to me most. Everything that should have been there was there and in the right size, the right shape, and the right places. This sweater provided cover but no concealment.

I was walking by and trying not to look or at least to be decently inconspicuous in my ogling. So again it was the girl who spoke.

"Mr. Erridge," she said. "We meet again. Good evening, Mr. Erridge."

I stopped and I returned her "Good evening." I had to leave it at that, since in the name department she had the advantage of me. I had no handle for her.

"Steve Dale—Matt Erridge."

The guy slid off the bridge rail and offered me his hand.

"Mr. Erridge, sir," he said.

I wasn't about to leave it that way with a generation gap unbridged. I took his hand.

"Mr. Dale, sir," I said. "I interrupted you."

"You did, didn't you?" he said.

"It doesn't matter. He'll pick up right where he left off. He never loses his place."

"May I ask a question?" I said.

"Of me or of him?" she asked.

"Either of you."

"Go ahead. One of us might even answer."

"Is it a his-and-her sweater? It's hard to believe there can be two of them."

"She knitted it for me," Dale said.

"And one for herself?"

"Just the one," she said. "We take turns wearing it. Tonight it's his turn."

"I just wanted to know. I can't imagine why, but I did want to know."

"Conversation piece," she said. "They're handy for awkward moments."

The meaning didn't escape me. The moment wasn't awkward of itself. Erridge was making it awkward.

"Nice seeing you again," I said, and to Dale it was: "Nice meeting you."

"See you around," he said.

She said nothing.

"Goodnight then," I said. "I'm keeping you from your work."

I took myself off. As I went, my head was full of speculation on other things they might be sharing besides the sweater. It was obvious that Dale was the man in possession. I tried hard not to be envious.

Although my first meeting with the girl had finished without promise, I had not been able to write it off as a closed episode. After this second encounter, however, I was convinced. It was quite possible that I would run into the girl again. Anything, after all, is possible, but the possible didn't include any expectation that it would ever come to anything. I would be batting out of my league, and she had made it all too clear that she wasn't even going to let me come up to the plate.

But then there was the third meeting, and that time I finally got to make the first move. It was the following morning and I had wakened with the feeling that I had been too long city-bound. The sun was shining. The sky was blue. The clouds—I don't think Dutch skies are ever free of clouds—were sun-gilded puffs of fluffy white.

I had an empty day ahead of me and I could think of nothing I could better do with the morning of it than fill it with a round of golf. It was going to be solitary golf, which may not be the best kind. It is, however, not the worst kind either.

Van Mieris had fixed me up with guest privileges at a

club not too far out of the city. When I dumped the golf bag into the Porsche and settled myself behind the wheel, I was looking forward to the drive or at least to that part of it which would come once I was free of the city traffic.

There is no city in the world where such freedom is easily won, but Amsterdam sets up special difficulties. There are the canals. Throughout the center traffic moves over narrow bridges and along the narrow roadways that flank most of the canals. That it moves at all is not much short of miraculous. You cannot expect it to move at much more than a pedestrian pace. It is not until you are out beyond the old city with its concentric rings of canals that you can begin to roll at even the slow pace of urban traffic in other places.

That morning I sweated out the crawl through the center, but then, after I had cleared that, I ran into an unexpected impediment. I had hit a good broad avenue that should have taken me straight out of town, but I had done no more than a few blocks of that before I was stuck with a detour. All traffic was being flagged off into a web of little streets where it again clogged and crawled.

It wasn't street excavation or any kind of construction that caused the detour. Even though the traffic was diverted to give the disturbance a wide berth, it was so noisy a disturbance that even at a distance of a couple of blocks there was no mistaking it. I could hear the yelling and the screaming. The yelling was enraged. The screaming was anguished.

There was also the smell. It was faint and it came and went with shifts in the breeze, but it was unmistakably the smell of battle, the reek of tear gas. At the distance of the detour it was too diluted to bring tears. For anyone who had ever taken a full-strength whiff of the stuff, however, it brought memory of tears. It was an easy guess, of course, that we were being detoured around some sort of riot. Who might be rioting and over what I had no way of knowing.

I was curious but not nearly enough to make a try at finding a place I could park the Porsche and walk in for a look. Even if my curiosity had been that great, there wouldn't have been a hope. Those little streets were solid with traffic, and the one through which I had Baby crawling was also solid with NO PARKING signs. It was far too narrow from curb to curb to permit any, and such cars as had been parked along it had been driven up on the sidewalk.

Inching my way along in the curb-to-curb jam, I saw the girl. My first thought was that it was her turn for the collision mat. She was wearing it and, if anything, she was looking even more a mess than that first time in the museum. Now her hair was spectacularly scrambled and, if she wasn't hysterical, she couldn't have been far from it.

She was standing at the curb down along a stretch of the street where an empty lot had itself hidden away behind a wooden construction fence. With what looked like desperation or at least panic she was trying to flag down a cab. No effort could have been more futile. Any cabs caught in that jam were occupied. Only an insane cabbie would have gone into that to cruise for fares.

I tried to get her attention, but it was hopeless. I leaned on Baby's horn, but that only inspired impatient drivers to lean on theirs. We were making the morning hideous with our blaring, but Baby's voice was lost in the raucous chorus. The girl just wasn't looking my way. I was, after all, not a taxi.

I had to wait till, inching along as much as the traffic

permitted, I had come abreast of where she was standing. Before I could reach her, however, I had several minutes during which I was close enough to see that she was crying. My first thought was that she had been caught in the tear gas, but, as I inched closer, it began to seem to me that this was not tear-gas crying.

Tear gas brings tears, blinding floods of the stuff. If you get enough of it, it will also have you gasping for air, but it's just gasping. It isn't sobbing. It's purely a physical reaction. It isn't emotional, and the kid's crying was conspicuously emotional. Her tears and sobs had been born of grief or rage, either or both, and aggravated by frustration.

As soon as I had come close enough, I threw Baby's door open.

"For now I'm a taxi," I said. "Jump in."

She gasped. It may have been astonishment or only trying to talk past a strangled sob.

"Yes," she said. "Yes, please."

I was certain that I had heard her right, but I had to wonder. She didn't jump in. Instead, she turned and ran away, squeezing herself through a small gap in the construction fence. It was no tight squeeze for her, but for the collision mat it was. The thing caught on a nail and had her hung up for a moment. Lunging through, she tore herself loose.

I wanted to get out of the car and go after her, but that way lay lynching. I had to stay with Baby to move her along each inch that might offer. You must remember that I was solidly wedged into that creeping mass of impatient and raging Dutchmen. So I just sat there moving ahead first one inch and then another.

The mass crawl had moved me along but not so much

that I wasn't still within easy reach when she came squeezing back through the fence. Close in her wake she was bringing Steve Dale. His curls were matted with blood and there were streaks of blood in the gold of his beard. From the waist up he was as good as naked. The tatters of ripped T-shirt that hung from his shoulders were covering not much of anything. I might have expected as much from what I had seen of his beard and his arms, but his chest was spectacularly hairy. There are guys on whom it grows that way. It looks like they have a doormat hanging down from their collarbones. The chest hair was also streaked with blood.

The girl was leading him. She could have been leading a blind and wounded bear.

I still had the car door standing open. I reached back and threw open the door in back. I expected that she would load him into the back and come and sit up front with me. She did load him in the back, but then she climbed in after him. She hadn't put him on the seat and she also ignored the seat. She had him lying on the floor and, settling down there herself, she took his bloody head into her lap. I reached over and pulled both doors shut.

"It'll be more comfortable for both of you up on the seat," I said.

"We're all right down here," she said. "Down here we may not be seen."

"You have been seen. There's everybody and his brother in this traffic jam and dozens of them have seen you. They can't have missed."

She moaned. "I know," she said, "but they're not the police. They may not do anything."

"The cops after him?"

"You can see what they did to him."

"I can see. I am aiding in the escape of a fugitive, or do I have an inflamed imagination?"

"I don't know."

All through this not too coherent exchange I was holding Baby to her place in the traffic crawl.

"You don't have to tell me anything you don't want to tell me," I said. "All I need to know is where I'm to take him, if I can ever get us out of this and on to something where we can roll, plus what I'm to say if we get stopped by the cops."

"Could you do something like vouching for him? Say something like you'll stand guarantor for his good behavior?"

It seemed like a good deal to ask when she wasn't telling me what his bad behavior had been. I had just said she didn't have to tell me anything she didn't want to tell me. Now I was trying to dream up the neatest way I could reverse myself on that. The wounded bear got in there before me.

"No," he said. "Nobody's making any promises for me."

"What makes you think the police would accept my guarantee?" I asked.

The question was one of those reaches for self-inflicted pain, like working at an injured place to see whether you can make it hurt. I was braced against her telling me I was an older man, venerable enough to win the respect of the police. She didn't say it. She took a far less wounding approach.

"Golf clubs," she began.

I had forgotten the golf bag.

"It's in your way," I said. "Just heave it up here on the seat beside me."

"No," she said. "We're all right. I meant the golf clubs

and your terrific car and your great clothes. All that makes you look like money and establishment and all that nonsense. Policemen are disgusting snobs. Confront them with a whiff of wealth and it's all kowtowing and touching forelocks. It's only with poor people that they're beastly. If you are both poor and young, you're one of the lower animals, made to be kicked."

"Stow it anyhow," Dale said. "I don't want anybody making any promises for me."

She ignored him.

"You probably won't have to guarantee anything," she said. "You won't even have to say anything."

"I just sit behind the wheel of my terrific car in my great clothes and look establishment? I don't think I can swing a golf club. No room for it."

"If we stay down out of sight and they see only you," she said, "they'll never think to stop you and look."

"He is on the lam?" I asked.

"I really don't know," she said. "Tear gas, fire hoses, even the clubs. They seemed to be trying to disperse the crowd, but when anyone fought back, they were making arrests."

"Steve fought back?"

"They wouldn't have come close enough to him to club him if he hadn't; but, you see, that's why I don't know. The idea was to disperse the crowd, or that's what it seemed like. So now he's dispersed. I should think they won't come after him, not if you can get him well away from all this."

"As soon as I can break out," I said. "But then where to? Nearest doctor? Nearest hospital?"

She answered with quick panic. "No doctor," she said. "No hospital. They'll tell the police."

He was cooler. "I don't need anything," he said. "All I need is to bathe the tear gas out of my eyes and wash away the blood. All I've got is a scalp cut. I'll wash it and put some iodine on it. I'll be okay."

"Where do I take you then?"

"My place," he said.

"No, better mine," the girl said.

"I'd like to get into this and say mine," I said. "The trouble is that I'm in a hotel and getting him through the lobby and up to my room wouldn't be what you could call private."

"Thanks," he said. "My place will do it."

"If the police come after you," the girl argued.

"How can they come after me? They don't know where I live."

"They did arrest some of the fellows. We don't know which or who."

"And you're thinking it may be some of the guys who know me and they'll turn me in? You don't know the guys then. They're my friends. They don't turn a friend in."

"You're not one of them, not as though you were one of their own. You're an American. No matter how close you've been with them, you're still something like an outsider. You don't belong, not the way they do."

"I'm a citizen of the world and they are citizens of the world. What about Sean and Whitey and Kraky? If I'm an outsider, they're outsiders too. Among us there are no outsiders."

"They're different. They're Europeans."

"So what are Americans like us if we're not ex-Europeans? Nobody cares where you were born. It's where you stand that counts."

"With you it does," she said.

"With them, too. I know them. We're like brothers. We stand together. We bleed together. We fight side by side. We trust each other."

"Comrades," I said.

It got me a snarl from the blood-smeared bear.

"I expected that," he said. "It's always the same simpleminded garbage. If a man doesn't stand with the oppressors, right away he's a Commie. I've got news for you, Mr. Erridge. They're oppressors too."

"Comrade is a good word," I said, "or it was until they took it over and loused up its meaning."

"Let's keep ideology out of this," the girl said. "Let's just be practical. We'll go to my place."

"I can't," he said. "It'll be like saying I don't trust the guys, and anyhow they know where you live."

She sighed. "There's no place," she said. "You're right. There's no place."

"There's my place," he insisted. "You can trust the guys."

"I'd like to be able to believe that," the girl said.

CHAPTER 2

He had, of course, been in the street riot. She had been in it, too, but I gathered only at the edges and only as an observer. He had been not only in the thick of it but fully exposed in the front line. She told me that much and, although her words were berating him for his stupidity, her tone contradicted the words. It was all pride.

He had stood up to the tear gas. He had not been hit with the pressure stream out of the fire hoses. That had been turned on the mass of the crowd while the police with their clubs beat down the few they'd isolated out front. The force of the water had driven the mass of the crowd back, and the police, charging past the fallen leaders, had moved forward in pursuit of the ones that hadn't been clubbed down.

That had been her moment for darting in, helping him to his feet, and pulling him away down a side street. Looking back, she had seen the others hauled up off the pavement and hustled to the police vans. Nobody had come after her and Dale.

I asked what it had been about, and I had my answer from Dale.

"Automobiles and people," he said.

"Which side were you on?" I asked.

"People," he said. "People matter. Automobiles are just things."

"Used by people," I said.

"People like you."

"And you."

I had to remind him of that.

"You can let me out," he said.

"Hush," the girl said. "Don't be a fool and don't be rude."

"It's okay," I said. "I'm not putting him out. I'm just wondering. What have the automobiles done to the people? What's the conflict?"

"It's housing," she explained. "There isn't enough. Working people and the poor with no place to live. They're tearing down houses to put up a big parking garage."

"They're not tearing down anything," Dale said. "They're going to be stopped."

"Maybe you stopped them today," she said, "but there will be other days."

"And we'll be there every time. They're not going to tear down anything without wading through our blood, and it will be with the whole world watching. That ties their hands—the whole world watching. It won't tie ours."

"You're an American," I said. "You may be living here now and you do have a place to live. It's where you want me to take you. What makes it your bind?"

"I am for people. What more should it take to make it my bind?"

"I don't know," I said. "You're a guest in this country. Guests are expected not to interfere in the affairs of their hosts."

"Expected?" he said. "When it's the weak fighting the strong, you can never win if you limit yourself to doing the expected."

We came down to a cross street where I could manage a turn out of the jam. I wasn't the only one taking it. Like me, other drivers may, even if for some less compelling reason, have given up on going where they had been headed. There would also have been others who were pulling out to go in search of some less clogged route.

So even when we were out of that thickest jam, we were still something less than in the clear. We were, however, at least moving, even though at no great clip. The time had come to ask directions.

Dale gave me an address. It was a street I didn't know.

"You'll have to guide me," I said.

The girl took over. "I'll sit up where I can see," she said. "Will you be all right down here, Steve? You have to stay down. It'll be no good if everyone we pass sees the blood on you."

"You've got some of my blood on you, Julie," he said.

That was the first I had anything like a name for her.

"Not so much as will be noticed," she said. She pulled herself up onto the back seat but, leaving him with his head no longer pillowed in her lap, she was worried about him. "You will be all right down there?" she asked.

"At your feet?" he said. "I know no better place."

She called him a fool, but it was another time when her tone gave her away.

She leaned forward to talk to me. "This isn't going to be easy," she said. "I don't know this part at all."

"Who does?"

"Steve does, but he has to stay down. Can you find the way back into the old city? Stadhouderskade, Wibaut-straat, Mauritskade—one of those streets and I'll be all right from there."

She was talking an area I knew, and I had a good enough line on the general direction in which it lay. I took the first available turn. That had us doubling back the way I had come before I hit the detour. I was doing it on a parallel street, but I had one on which the traffic, for city traffic, was tooling along nicely.

I couldn't have hit a better street. It took us straight into the museum district and, even before we had come that far, she had begun picking up landmarks she knew. She guided me into a small street right close to the museums. It was in the part of town I knew, although I had never before been in this particular small byway and I hadn't known it by name.

It was a good street, solidly lined with the narrow-fronted, tall houses that are old Amsterdam. They all had the gabled tops with the big hook sticking out just below the peak of the eaves. All those narrow-fronted jobs have narrow doors, and inside their stairs are all steep and narrow. For people who built their houses that way the old Dutch had an inconvenient taste for furniture that was big and solid. Big chests, broad beds, huge tables—there was never a chance you could get them in the front door or up the narrow stairs.

That was why the hooks. Anything that was good Dutch size had to be brought in or out by block and tackle, hoisted in through the windows. All the houses along that little street were in a beautiful state of repair. They had the look of places that had been lived in and cared for down through the centuries. These houses hadn't been allowed to fall into neglect and later been pulled back by restoration. No matter how well that's done, it shows. You can see it.

So it was a street of solid affluence, and the cars parked

along the curb further attested to it. A Mercedes, BMWs, a Bentley, a Cadillac, and never so much as a scratch on any of them. The one exception was a small panel truck.

I wasn't at all sure that I was going to be asked in. By this time I knew Julie well enough to recognize that at dismissing Erridge she was a great hand. I hoped that Dale was going to need a lot of help. I was curious to see his place. I had long since gathered that he wasn't homeless. Now it looked as though he couldn't be poor either.

She told me where to pull up. Completely in command, she told Dale to stay where he was, out of sight.

"I'll get the door open," she said. "Then Matt will bring you in. He'll do it just as quickly as he can. With luck, nobody will see you."

"I can do it on my own," Dale said.

"With help you'll do it faster."

She went to the door and fished a latchkey out of her purse. They had spoken of her place and his place. I had rather liked hearing that, but if she carried a key to his, it could be assumed that he had a key to hers.

"None of your business, Erridge," I told myself.

She opened the door and gave me the nod. I was already out of the car and standing by. Dale was also at the ready. I opened the car door and he came tumbling out. I only just managed to catch him. He sagged in my grasp.

"You're worse off than you're admitting, my lad," I was thinking, but I wasn't wasting any breath on saying it.

I was more than half carrying him as I rushed him into the house and kicked the front door shut behind us. Julie had gone on up the stairs. I started him up after her. On the stairs—and being Amsterdam stairs, they were murderously steep—I had expected that I would have to end up slinging him over my shoulder and carrying him.

With every step, however, he was coming to be more on his own. The collapse into my arms hadn't been anything. Lying cramped all that time on the floor of the Porsche, he had stiffened up and, on first try, his legs hadn't been up to supporting him. Those crazy stairs were limbering him up fast.

It was no easy climb, five long flights all the way to the top of the house. Julie was up there holding his door open. Obviously, she had a key to that one too, but that was nothing to think about. She would hardly have had the one without the other. Once we were inside his flat, all that went out of my mind.

I was confronted with some quite different food for thought. It was a studio, one big room under the slant of the roof. There was a big skylight through which on this bright morning sunlight flooded the room even to its farthest corners. For any purposes of living the furniture was so sparse as to be Spartan.

There was no bed, only a mattress on the floor in one corner. That appeared to be the living corner. It had a well-filled bookshelf, a reading lamp, and a couple of chairs. At the back of the place there was a small dressing room lined with drawers and closets, and beyond it a glisteningly modern bathroom. I later saw another small room, a little pocket of kitchen, also glitteringly modern.

Since the first order of business was washing away blood and dealing with Steve's scalp cut, we herded straight through to the bathroom. Julie tried her hand at the Florence Nightingale bit, but it was quickly obvious that she had neither the aptitude nor the experience for it. I took over. I wanted to shave a patch of his scalp, but he didn't own anything like a razor. I had to make do with a small scissors gadget I had in my pocketknife to cut away enough hair to bring the damage into view.

It wasn't anything much to worry about. He was building a couple of good lumps and, although the scalp had bled plentifully, there was nothing there that with washing and disinfecting couldn't be expected to take over on its own to mend itself.

I took care of that part of it while Julie kept laying wet cloths on the patient's eyes. All this time we were out in the bathroom working on him, I was carrying a headful of questions.

I've told you about only the smallest and least important part of what I had seen while passing through the big room. There was only that one corner for living. The rest of the acreage was workspace, and about that there was nothing makeshift. There was a large and elaborate setup of track lighting. There was a big turntable. There was a long counter on which was set out a great array of tools—knives, scrapers, mallets, chisels, long instruments of pale wood for which I had no name. There was also an all-pervading smell of clay.

This Steve Dale, then, was a sculptor. Either he was eminently successful—he could have been, even though I had never heard of him—or else he was extraordinarily well-heeled through other sources of revenue. This was not the attic in which the struggling young artist worked and starved. All of that was interesting but it was hardly baffling. He wouldn't be the first lad financed by Daddy through the early stages of a career in the arts.

There was something else that I had seen in passing, and it was this something else that filled my head with questions. Ranged neatly on the counter along with the tools were six plaster heads. All six were alike, evidently all cast from the same mold.

I was guessing that they were an example of Dale's work. They weren't pretty. They were savage and they were clever. They were caricatures and they had been made just as nasty as they could be within the bounds of the recognizable. The clay could have been molded into so monstrous a satire only if the work had been fueled by hate.

The plaster of some of the heads was painted, and the color had been applied with a skilled malice that was easily the equal of what had gone into the modeling. Since I had noticed that one of the heads had been painted only in part, I gathered that it was a work in progress. That one was to be finished, and the other blankly white ones would be waiting for their coloring.

I have said that for all their nastiness they were within the bounds of the recognizable. It was that about them that had filled my head with questions. I recognized the model. I had dined with the man the night before. He hadn't been my host, only a fellow guest.

I hadn't liked his face. Too beefy, it had the look of the indecently well-fed. Furthermore, it wasn't the kind of face that should have had the small, steely eyes or the rat-trap mouth. Now there he was out there on the counter, readily recognizable even though exaggerated into something a Gothic stonecutter might have done for a frieze of the Seven Deadly Sins. This was Avarice, multiplied by six.

I waited till I had finished with the head wounds and was winding some kind of a head bandage around the curls, before I said anything.

"Dorstman?" I said.

"Fredrik the Gross," Dale said. "You know him?"

"I was just coming away from dinner with him when I ran into the two of you last night."

A quick freeze set in. It came off the two of them like the breath off a glacier.

"You keep all kinds of company," Dale said.

"I fall into things," I said. "I wouldn't know you if it hadn't been for Julie. I wouldn't know Fredrik Dorstman if I hadn't been asked to a dinner where he was a fellow guest."

"Then you'll want to fall out of this thing," Dale said.

Julie protested. "Steve," she said. "He's been kind and he certainly didn't have to be. You're being ungracious and ungrateful."

"Not at all," Dale said. "They were his own words. He fell into it. He didn't know what he was falling into. He doesn't want to be mixed up with the likes of me." He dropped off into one of those eloquent pauses. It dripped significance. Then he pulled the trigger. "Unless," he said, "he does want just that and he didn't fall into anything. He knew where he was going all along."

"Now, just what does that mean?" Julie asked.

"If he doesn't know what it means," Dale said, "then he'll want no part of me. If he knows, he'll understand that I want no part of him."

"I hope that's just from being knocked on the head," Julie said. "You should apologize."

"Baby," Dale said, "this isn't some drawing-room comedy. It's war."

"You're being stupid."

"Maybe I am. In war you do stupid things. You have to. That's the way war is."

"And a man has to keep his guard up against spies and infiltrators," I said.

"That's ridiculous."

She was trying hard but there was a noticeable lack of

conviction in her protests. The words were good enough, but they were only words. She had no certainty that he was wrong. She just wanted him to be polite.

"Of course, it's ridiculous," I said. "It's counterespionage, and there's only the one thing you can count on in counterespionage. It falls into farce."

"And Mr. Erridge," Dale said, "is very big in falling into."

"That's perceptive," I said. "It's remarkable on such short acquaintance. Anyhow, let's keep it short. I don't think there's anything more I can do for you. Your head's going to be all right."

"The outside of it," Julie said.

"Nothing I can do for the inside, so I'll be on my way. You do a great grotesque, Dale. Sometime I'd like to see what you could do with love."

"Thanks," Dale said. "Thanks for everything. Maybe I'm wrong. I hope I'm wrong. I'd like to like you."

"It's all right," I said. "Don't strain yourself." I turned to Julie. "It is all right," I said.

"You've been wonderfully kind," she said. "I appreciate it. I'll go down with you."

"I can find the way," I said. "It's easy, only the one way to go."

She came down the stairs with me, valiantly trying to make amends.

"Steve isn't himself," she said. "He's upset and it has him all mixed up. He's a sweet boy."

"Who hates himself," I said.

"What makes you say that?"

"He can only love the poor," I said. "Obviously, he isn't poor, so he's in trouble with himself."

"He doesn't hate himself. He just hates the money. He

spends practically nothing on himself, only on his work, and he's always giving money away."

"Where does it come from?" I asked.

"Oh," she said, "it's always been there."

"It came from somewhere."

"His grandfather, his grandmother. He has nobody. Everybody's dead, and he's been left with everybody's money."

"And everybody's guilt."

"I suppose so. He says he hates to think about how it was made. Strikebreakers. Lockouts. Pinkerton thugs. It was all way back before he was even born, but he's always thinking about it."

"Was it made that way?" I asked.

"Who knows?" she said. "According to Steve, there was no other way it could have been made, no other way the big gobs of money ever have been made."

"I don't know," I said. "Right in his own line of work—the arts—didn't Picasso die many times a millionaire?"

She giggled. "I'll have to ask him about that," she said. "Of course, there weren't any Picassos in his family. It was steel and railroads and things like that."

That much talk had taken us down to the front door. On the doorstep we ran into a man. He was wearing the uniform—tight jeans, baggy sweat shirt, sandals. Although he wasn't old, he wasn't quite young enough for the look he was trying to achieve. It made him look a little ridiculous. He was a big guy, though, with a lot of muscle on him.

I put him at an age when on most guys the muscle begins to give way to fat. It happens often in the thirties, but it hadn't been happening to him. He looked to be in good fighting shape.

Without taking time out for even the briefest greeting, he asked if Steve was upstairs. Before she answered, Julie did the introductions. That was a great girl for the proprieties.

"Matt," she said, "this is Piet Claes. Piet, Matthew Erridge."

He gave it no more than a breezy "Hi" and switched right back to his question.

"Steve up there?" he asked again.

"Yes."

"He okay?"

"He got clubbed some, but it looked worse than it was. He's all right."

"He shouldn't have been there," Claes said.

"You know Steve. Try and keep him away."

"But it's stupid. The world's full of heads that weren't made for much but breaking. Steve's too valuable."

"Go upstairs and tell him that."

"I ought to go up there and whip his britches."

I was saying nothing, though I was thinking it mightn't be a bad idea.

"I wouldn't try it if I were you," Julie said. "He's not in his sweetest mood today."

"And I'm not either," Claes said as he went into the house.

"Are you ever?" Julie asked the question of the empty air.

She went through a few more apologetic motions. I pulled the Porsche out of there and took off. I had killed the morning but I couldn't say it hadn't been interesting. It was an easy switch of schedule to an afternoon of golf. I could get lunch at the club and have a full afternoon out there ahead of me. I set off on the way I had gone in the morning. There was no chance that I would run into another riot. It would be too soon for that. Broken heads would have to mend first. Time would be needed for regrouping.

I had an easy run, contending with no more than normal traffic. I ran into no detour. In the second block beyond the corner where I had been turned away I spotted the scene of the morning's rioting. Pavements and building fronts were still wet.

When water is delivered in the quantities that come out of pressure hoses, it takes time before all of it will have gone away. Also, there was the line of boarded-up houses. They looked empty but it was a good bet that there would be squatters in them.

When housing is short, and nobody was making a secret of the fact that in Amsterdam housing for the poor was very short, nothing that even resembles shelter goes unoccupied. That row of houses bore only a remote resemblance to shelter. Nobody could live in those old wrecks decently, but people who cannot manage decently manage as they can. I had in my time seen too many of the shantytowns of the world not to recognize that those ruins were several cuts better than the average for such.

There were signs fixed to some of the house fronts. I have no Dutch, but they had the look of such signs the world over. The buildings were marked for demolition. The signs were liberally scrawled with graffiti. I didn't need any Dutch to know that they would be the customary obscenities. Also they were illustrated. The drawings could hardly have been from Steve Dale's hand. Any filthy pictures he might have drawn would have been more skillfully done. The illustrations were without any trace of talent.

I made it out to the golf club. I had lunch. I went around in more strokes than you need to know about and I drove back into town, getting in late in the afternoon. The hotel desk had a message for me.

Julie Grant had called. Would Mr. Erridge please call her as soon as he came in? She had left a number. I tried to remember whether I had ever mentioned the name of my hotel. I was certain that I hadn't. Amsterdam has hundreds of hotels. Could she have been calling one after the other till she'd hit the right one? On my way up to my room I amended that. You could cut it down to the kinds of hotels she would have expected me to have chosen, and then it wouldn't be hundreds anymore. It would still have been more than a few. Also, it was my guess that she would have started with the big, flashy, brand-new, international-type jobs. That would be where she would expect an American in town on business to stay. She could hardly have known that I like my foreign places to be foreign and that I wouldn't be in any of the big-chain jobs.

It was with some uneasiness that I dialed the number that she had left for me. The voice of caution was telling me that there was something here that wasn't completely aboveboard, but when a Julie Grant calls, breathes there the man with lusts so dead that he heeds the voice of caution?

She came on quickly. I had visions of her sitting by the phone and grabbing it up at the first tinkle.

"Julie," I said. "Matt. I have a message. You called me."

"Yes, Matt. You asked me to have dinner with you."

"It seems like a long time ago," I said.

"The day we first met. Have you forgotten?"

"How could I forget that you said a firm no?"

"I'm slow, Matt. You'll have to forgive me for it. To-night? Or are you tied up?"

"You bringing Steve?" I asked.

"Steve will be lying down with ice on his head."

"And you don't stand by to keep the ice replenished?"

"I've done my share of standing by for this day. I've earned a break."

"Dinner with me is a break?"

"That's false modesty," she said. "You know you're good company."

"Where do I pick you up? At Steve's?"

"No. I'm home. It's too much trouble telling you how to find it. We can meet in your hotel lobby."

"All I need is the address. I'm old-fashioned. I call for girls. They don't call for me. A taxi will find the way."

"I hate taxis," she said. "I want to ride in your lovely Porsche."

"We don't have to keep the taxi all evening, just to bring us back to Baby."

"Who's Baby?"

"The Porsche. She's the love of my life, but don't tell Steve. He's anti-automobile."

"Not really. He's just pro-people."

"Are we going to spend the evening talking about him?"

"You brought him up."

"I guess I did. So now I'm dropping him. Address?"

She came through with it and we set the time. I show-ered and shaved. I toyed with the idea of a sweater and jeans, but the thought that I might look even a little bit like Piet Claes stopped me cold. I opted for something that was more myself—shirt, tie, slacks, coat—decently sober but not too sober.

Down at the hotel desk I got the clerk to locate the address for me on the city map. It didn't look all that difficult. It was another of those little streets and it was only around the corner from Steve Dale's studio. Tooling around there in Baby, I learned that it wasn't as easy as it looked. I had to deal with a flock of one-way-street problems, coming into it from the least reasonable direction.

Baby, however, was up to the challenge. We bent some speed limits, making the circuit, but we pulled up at Julie's door at the appointed time. She was ready. Don't ask me what she was wearing. It was a dress, soft and sleek, the kind of dress that seems to say nothing about itself and everything about what it has inside it.

This was another Julie Grant. It wasn't the girl of the collision mat and it wasn't the sweater-and-skirt type. It was a Julie Grant nicely concocted for Matt Erridge's delectation. I couldn't help thinking a Mata Hari but only in the most ladylike way.

I had my moment of triumph. I was so clever to have found the way. She piled it on.

"You're pretty clever yourself," I said. "How did you find me? I'm sure I never happened to tell you where I was staying."

"Not clever at all. You're Matthew Erridge. Matthew Erridges can't hide."

"What does *that* mean?"

"Don't you read the papers?"

"What papers?"

"The local papers. The Dutch papers."

"I'm ignorant. I can't read Dutch."

"There was a piece about you. Eminent engineer arrives in Amsterdam. Speculation about what great project is afoot. It gave the name of your hotel."

A likely story. I wasn't believing a word of it, even though it was not impossible. In any case, I had her riding along beside me and I wasn't going to let any lack of faith spoil the evening. I did expect that sometime in the course of it there would be that question or two to probe after some intelligence she might carry back to Steve Dale, but there was nothing like that.

We had dinner, and after dinner we went on to a jazz club that was like most European jazz clubs. They take their Dixieland seriously over there, even solemnly. It was well after midnight when she said that she'd had a long and exhausting day. She'd loved the evening. I was a great dear and would I now, please, take her home.

Riding back to her place, she was like a kid past her bedtime. She even fell asleep on my shoulder. She didn't wake when I pulled up, and when I put my arm around her and nestled her more snugly against me she just made some little cooing sound and went on sleeping. I sat in the car with her and let her sleep. She seemed so trusting that she had me feeling incongruously parental.

The small panel truck I'd noticed when we brought Dale home—or one just like it—was now parked here, around the corner in Julie's street. Again it was a standout on that curbside lined with the shiny superjobs.

When she stirred and began to wake, she was irresistible. I brought her full awake with a kiss. Then, when she was awake, she let me kiss her some more, and then it wasn't just a wake-up kiss. It was more serious. She came out of it saying she would be falling asleep in my arms again and she mustn't do that. I asked her why not. She said she mustn't because she was exhausted and it wouldn't be sufficiently restful.

I saw her inside and up to the door of her flat. She

kissed me goodnight there. She wasn't asking me in. I didn't push it. I had her address and I had her phone number. I had the hope of other evenings. Back behind Baby's wheel, however, I was telling myself not to count on it. How could I expect that there would be another evening when Steve Dale would be lying down with ice on his head? Another part of me came in and told me that I could expect it. I could well imagine that Dale might have a permanent relationship with billy clubs.

I managed the one-way-street deal and drove Baby around to the garage where I was keeping her stowed. That was the small price I paid for my preference for a Dutch hotel. The big new international jobs have garage space for their patrons right at hand. My hotel had none, but it was no big deal. It was about a five-minute drive between the hotel and the garage, but that was the one-way streets again.

Walking over to pick Baby up or walking back to the hotel after depositing her, I had almost no walk at all, only a couple of footbridges over a couple of canals and I was there.

I was just coming up on my first footbridge when I had it. I was in a dark patch where a parked panel truck cast its shadow. The hit came at me out of nowhere. Allow me a cliché: I never knew what hit me. There's no other way to say it. I know I was hit because, in the first place, I'm not a guy who just comes down with a sudden attack of the vapors. In the second place, I came out of it in need of exactly the kind of attention I had given Steve Dale that morning. I'd been hit on the head and with scalp-lacerating force. The blow had been well placed, neatly located for knocking me cold.

CHAPTER 3

How long I was out I don't know. I never thought of checking my watch when I came to. We've all seen those India-rubber heroes of movies and TV. They're knocked cold and they come out of it bouncing right back, possessed of undiminished vigor and with their senses and thinking immediately returned to full competence. In case you don't know, you can take the word of a guy who's been there. Coming back out of it is a gradual process.

Consciousness comes back and competence follows after it, but then only in a slow ooze. The dream merchants who invent those bouncing rubber heroes do it out of a happy innocence. They have never themselves been knocked cold.

I came out of it, but only in that all-too-human way that is Erridge's way. I opened my eyes but only to blink them. I shook my head in an effort to work myself loose from the constellations that had invaded it. As I lay there on the footbridge, I was attempting nothing more strenuous than that. I was waiting for the time when my legs would begin feeling as though they could hold me.

I was lying on the bridge and I had no memory of having reached it. I turned my head to look back to where I'd been when I last remembered. I couldn't locate the spot.

The parked truck I could have used for orientation was no longer there.

Even then I didn't leap to my feet equipped for any great deeds of derring-do. I pulled myself up by the bridge rail, and then I rested there for some moments bent over the rail while my dinner reached a decision on whether or not it was going to stay down. For several of those moments I can describe it only as irresolute. In what seemed like very slow stages it began telling me that it was going to settle back down where I had put it.

It was during that time that, bent over the bridge rail, I saw the thing afloat in the canal. It looked like a man and he was floating face down. As I saw it then, it could have been the body of a man who had drowned, or it could have been a drowning man.

What I might have done if I had been in full possession of my faculties I cannot say. Even at my best I am not always wise. All too often I move without stopping to think. If all my senses had been in better shape, I might have seen the thing differently, but there again I don't know. I pulled back from the rail, I skinned out of my coat, and I kicked out of my shoes.

I climbed up on to the rail and I dove into the canal. It was Erridge to the rescue. Let's face it, however, it was a fuddled Erridge. The water in that canal was cold. The shock of it did much toward bringing me back to my senses. I swam a few strokes and got my hands on the thing. At first touch I knew that it wasn't a person. It had clothes on, but inside the clothes it was a thing.

It was light. Dead or alive, flesh and bone are never so light. It yielded to the touch as even the softest flesh will never yield. It felt like straw. I can offer only the excuse of my fuddled state for what I did about it. I worked at rescuing the thing. I took a firm hold on it and swam with it to the bank of the canal. I handled it just as I would have if I had been endeavoring to save a drowning man. I suppose I wasn't thinking. Some old habit out of lifesaving drills had taken over.

At the edge of the canal I had problems. There was no such easily negotiable convenience as a sloping bank. It was a stone retaining wall and it rose a good three feet above the level of the water. I could find nothing on the surface of the wall that would give me any kind of hand grip. The stone was slimy. It was slick with moss.

There I was treading water and idiotically hanging on to the thing with one hand while futilely groping with the other for something I could grab for pulling my burden and me up out of the canal. While I was working at it, an appreciation of my situation did dawn on me. It came, however, as the dawn comes, only gradually, but it was a dawn that carried no promise of any sudden burst of sunrise.

When the two guys popped up above me at the top of the wall and started shouting down to me, their shouting meant nothing. That took another of those slow dawns before I got to the place where I shouted back at them. I came up with some of the few words of Dutch I'd found it necessary to know in that country where almost everyone speaks some English. I asked them if they understood English.

They did and they switched to it. They were going to lower a rope and they wanted me to fasten it around the waist of my burden. The rope came down. I grabbed it with my free hand and, letting go of my burden, I started fastening it around my own waist.

"No, no," they yelled. "Him first. You after."

"Not a *him*," I yelled back. "An *it*."

I should have found a better way of putting it. That was too tricky a thing to ask them to grasp in a language that was not their own. I ignored their instructions and finished fastening the rope around myself. The thing meanwhile was drifting away from me. With the rope around me I swam a stroke or two and gathered it back in.

"Not the both of you at once," they were shouting. "It's too heavy. Him first and then you."

"Not too heavy," I shouted back. "It weighs next to *nothing*."

I had a firm grip on the thing and I waited for them to haul me up. I could hear them up there talking it over, but their voices were lowered for that and they were talking in Dutch. I could make nothing of it. After talking it over between themselves, they must have concluded that they were stuck with me and I would have to be humored.

I felt the slack go out of the rope. They began hauling me up. Almost at once, even while they were pulling, they broke out in an excited jabber. It was Dutch jabber. I couldn't understand a word of it, but it was an easy guess that they were knocked over by the discovery that the combined weight of what looked like two big men could add up to so little.

As soon as they had me within reach, they grabbed my burden away from me. One of them was holding the rope while the other was lifting the thing to the top of the wall. For a moment the rope went slack and I slid back a few feet down the moss-greasy wall, but then they were pulling again and they brought me to the top.

Perhaps I should have been having some thoughts

about who the two guys would be, but that just hadn't come into my mind. It was only when they had me standing dripping before them that I first recognized that they were two policemen. I also recognized that they were something less than friendly. I detected a total lack of sympathy. Nothing, in fact, seemed to be coming at me but suspicion and stern disapproval. It occurred to me that officers of the law should have been showing at least some small measure of concern for a man with a bloody head. By then, however, I had attained a sufficient level of rationality to bring me around to a quick revision of that judgment.

I had been down in the canal. I was guessing that the water had washed the blood away. Even if there was still some flow of it, there would be an interval before it would show again.

"All right, mister," one of the cops said. "What's the silly game?"

"I don't know," I said. "It's no game of mine."

"You better explain."

"I made the same mistake as you did," I said. "I saw it in the water. It looked like a man. If he wasn't already drowned, he was in trouble. I went into the canal to help him."

Now, standing over it where they had laid it on the pavement, I could see that it was exactly what I had assumed—a dummy made of straw and dressed in old clothes. It could have been a scarecrow except that you'd have to make an exception of the head. I had never seen a scarecrow where anyone took much trouble over fabricating the head.

The head of this dummy, much the worse for submersion, was still easily recognizable. It was a head of painted plaster. Some of the plaster had crumbled off it and some of the paint had run, but if it wasn't one of those six duplicates of the Dorstman head I'd seen in Dale's studio, it would have been a seventh casting of the same work.

My clothes were dripping water and my hair was streaming with it. It kept running down into my eyes and I was dashing it away with the back of my hand. Abruptly it came to me that it wasn't only water I was wiping away. It was blood as well. Whether the officers noticed it on their own or I called it to their attention by my stupid staring at the red on my hand, they did a quick switch in their line of questioning.

"You're hurt," one of them said.

The other one suggested that in the course of my misguided rescue attempt I had somehow hit my head. I set them right on that, giving them a quick fill-in on what I've already told you. It wasn't a complete fill-in. I said nothing about Julie and nothing about Steve Dale or the plaster heads I had seen in his studio.

One of them stood by with the dummy while the other went up on the bridge with me. I showed him where I had been when I came to. The place, after all, was marked. It was where I had left my shoes and coat. They were still where I had dropped them before going into the canal. There was also some of my blood there.

I located for the cop the place where I'd been hit. There were smears of my blood there as well. Back on the bridge I picked up the shoes and the coat. I had no intention of putting them on. I was much too wet for that. At the suggestion of the officer, however, I checked my coat pockets. As both he and I had expected, my wallet was gone. I set about checking for anything else that might have been taken, but nothing else was missing. While I was going through pockets, though, the cop came up with my wallet. He found it on the pavement at the far end of the bridge.

When he handed it to me, I checked it out. Everything was where it should have been—credit cards, driver's license, and such—everything but the money. All interest switched away from the straw man with the plaster head. It was now just foreign visitor assaulted and robbed, a matter for considerable regret and great shame.

They took on about it in such a big way that it came around to the place where I was comforting them. It was not their estimable country. It was the state of the world. Such things happened everywhere. Certainly they knew that even my own country, the United States, was not immune. I assured them that I hadn't lost much.

I had spent almost all of the money I'd had on me that evening. I had not been far from moving into the credit cards when Julie had called it a night. So it had been only a paltry haul for the mugger, no more than a few guilders. I couldn't offer any exact count, but I knew it had been no more than would have translated into twenty bucks or less.

At first they took that as making the crime more heinous. They seemed to be horrified by the idea that anyone would club a man senseless for so paltry a haul. I suppose I should have kept my mouth shut. It shouldn't have bothered me that they were taking it so hard.

"He had no way of knowing he was going to be disappointed," I said.

They looked at each other and then they looked at me. The one who had stayed with the straw man spoke first.

"He didn't have to be disappointed," he said. "He could have taken your watch. It's a good watch."

The second cop agreed on the watch, but he had his own contribution to make. He was the one who had retrieved my wallet for me and he had been with me when I'd been checking out my pockets.

"And your cigarette lighter," he said. "A gold cigarette lighter at today's price of gold . . ."

I made a try at laughing it off.

"Let's not mourn about it," I said. "I can't regret his overlooking them."

They were not only an observant pair, but they were bright as well. At that moment I had the beginnings of a feeling that was to grow. In my situation I would have preferred a pair of uniformed dullards.

"He was in a hurry," one of them said.

"He didn't have the whole of his mind for the robbery," the second one said.

"Did he have the games to play with the dummy?" the other one asked.

I shrugged it off. It was their problem. I wasn't going to say or do anything to promote the thought that it might be mine as well.

Although I assured them I didn't need it, they loaded me into their squad car and took me to the nearest hospital. The medics and the nurses did nothing for me that I couldn't have done for myself, although I wouldn't have gone through any of that business of holding fingers up in front of my eyes and counting them or of testing out my knee jerks, and I wouldn't have taken my blood pressure or given myself a tetanus shot.

Hospitals, however, have their routine and, once you're in their hands, it's simplest just to go along. I'll give them this: they did a neater head bandage than I would have done for myself. I had done my best for Steve Dale, and my best just didn't measure up.

For all of this they'd had me in one of those hospital gowns, and by the time they were ready to turn me loose a couple of hours had gone by and they were able to return my clothes to me thoroughly dried. Nothing was pressed, and there were dried residues that indicated that Amsterdam's canal water is conspicuously rich in suspended solids.

I had a taxi back to my hotel. By then it was that hour before dawn when I had only the night porter as a lobby audience for my arrival. He was more than enough. He was all solicitude, but it took the form of a bombardment of questions. It was all too complicated to explain and I was not at all certain that I wanted to explain. I took the easy way.

"I fell into a canal," I said. "I've been to the hospital and I'm all right. I feel all right and they said in the hospital that I am all right."

That little speech served its purpose. It knocked off the questions. Of course, it won me a peculiar look, guarded but peculiar. It's the mark of a good hotel for it to have a staff that can give suave acceptance to the oddities of the patrons, even to the extreme oddities of an American abroad. The day man would probably have taken it with even smoother aplomb.

Up in my room I stripped down and did a thorough scrub under the shower. They had done a great clean-up on me at the hospital but, after even the short taxi ride in those clothes, I had great need of another.

By the time I had dried myself, I had every bone and muscle telling me it was bedtime, but I couldn't make my head concur. I couldn't trust myself on the bed. Even sitting on the edge of it I would have weakened and succumbed to the sheets. I pulled on a fresh pair of shorts. Everything I'd been wearing would be going to valet service as soon as such hotel facilities would be coming awake.

Dragging a chair over to the bedside table, I perched on that and picked up the phone. I dialed Julie's number. It was no time to be calling anybody but I couldn't see that I had a choice. It took a lot of ringing before there was any response, and then it was both sleepy and indignant. There was no "Hello." There was no "Julie Grant here." She came on in what the literature profs back in my college days had taught me was called *in medias res*.

"I don't know who you are," she said, "and I don't think I want to know, because, whoever you are, you're insane."

She sounded like a woman who was about to hang up on me, but she wasn't hanging up. I couldn't say she sounded as though she had been expecting a call, but, for all her indignation, she sounded as though she wasn't too astonished at having one.

"Matt Erridge," I said.

That brought on a marked change of tone. The indignation was still there, but something guarded and cautious had come into it.

"Do you know what time it is?" she asked.

"A terrible time to be calling anybody," I said. "I didn't want to wake you, but I have to have Steve Dale's number and I don't think it can wait."

That changed it again. She was still coming through guarded and cautious, but now it was tremulous as well.

"What do you want with him?" she asked.

"Just to tell him something he ought to know."

"You can tell me."

"It may be a problem, Julie, but if it is, it's not your problem. It's his."

"You'll have to tell me."

"Have to?"

"It'll be the only way you can get the word to him. I'm not giving you his number."

"Okay," I said. "Sorry I woke you. I'll get it from information or I'll go around to the studio."

"Matt, don't be like that. Please don't be like that."

"Like what?"

"Oh, you know. Difficult—hostile."

"Aren't you the one who's being difficult?"

"I'm thinking of you, Matt."

"That's nice," I said, "because I'm thinking of you. I smell trouble, Julie, and I'm not about to put you into it."

"Don't worry about me, Matt. I'll be all right."

"That's what you think," I said. "I'm not that sure."

"Yesterday morning?" she said. "I didn't do anything but pull Steve away, and if it happens again and I can do it again, I'll do it. If you want to tell Steve not to let me know when there's going to be another demonstration, you don't have to do it now. There won't be another this soon. Also, telling him will do no good. You can't get a crowd for a demonstration without putting the word out. So how will anybody manage to keep me from getting the word?"

"Julie," I said because I had come to feel that she was asking for it. "There were those heads Steve had in the studio. Six of them in plaster, all from the same mold."

"A joke," she said.

"I saw one of them tonight, and nobody was laughing."

"You couldn't have," she said, and there was a lot of gasp in the way she said it. "You were . . ."

Those last two words slipped out. From the way she broke it off there, I could tell that she wanted to have them back.

"I was what?"

She had stuck her neck out. I wasn't going to let her pull it back in.

"You were with me all evening. We were together all the time. You couldn't have seen anything I didn't see, and we were nowhere near . . ."

It was becoming chronic. Again there were the few words that escaped her.

"Nowhere near what?" I asked.

The answer was too slow in coming. She was obviously searching her mind for some safe way out. When she came up with it, she threw it at me with more vehemence than conviction.

"We were nowhere near the studio," she said.

It was as though she might have been asking me an unspoken question. She couldn't believe that I had seen the thing. Certainly she didn't want to believe it. On the other hand, she was beginning to have some difficulty in believing that I might be lying about it. She was trying to fight off being forced to accept the possibility, but it wasn't any good. She had to know.

"And when I left you," I said, "that was the nearest I came to the studio. I drove straight out of the neighborhood."

"You saw it after you left me?" she asked. "You've just seen it? You went down there?"

They were questions, but they didn't sound like questions. They were accusations.

"Down where?" I asked.

"Don't play games with me, Matt." Now she was storming. She was snarling at me. The anger in her voice was the least of it. There was also contempt. "You know very well where," she said. "I was just humoring Steve, but I wouldn't believe it. I thought he was being stupid, but I was the stupid one. Steve was right about you."

"Maybe you know what you're talking about, kid," I said. "I don't. After I left you, I drove around to the garage and turned my car in. I was walking to the hotel from the garage. By one of the footbridges some guy came up behind me and knocked me on the head. When I came to, he had dragged me onto the bridge and he had taken the few guilders I had on me, hardly enough to be worth cracking my head for."

"Where are you now?"

All the anger and contempt were gone. They had been replaced by solicitude, and I was certain it was not an act. It rang true.

"In my hotel."

"I'll throw on some clothes. I'll be right over. Have you had a doctor?"

"A whole flock of them. The police insisted on taking me to a hospital. The doctors gave me the works. They tried very hard to find something wrong with me and they couldn't."

"Did you tell them that you saw the head?" she asked.

I misread the question. I thought that she was afraid that I might have told them.

"I haven't told anyone anything. That's why I have to talk to Dale right away."

"You should have told the doctors," she said.

"What does that mean?" I asked.

"You had your head cracked open. You were knocked unconscious. With a thing like that you don't hold anything back from the doctors. You never know. It can be serious. They should know that you are seeing things."

"Julie, come on! It isn't seeing things, not in the way you're saying it. The cops who took me to the hospital saw it too. They have it. Nobody cracked them on the head."

"What are you?" she asked. "CIA? What?"

So now we had doubled back. It was anger and contempt all over again.

"Look," I said, "let's not be silly."

"Let's not," she said. "You took the police down there. When I think that I let you kiss me . . ."

"Down where?" I tried again.

"We're not playing that game anymore," she said. "You know perfectly well where."

"I know perfectly well. It was on that footbridge over the canal. I was knocked cold. I came out of it and I saw what looked like a man down in the canal. I was stupid enough to jump in to pull him out. It wasn't a man. It was a straw dummy, but its head was one of those jobs of Steve's."

"In the canal near your hotel?"

"A block away."

"What was it doing there?"

"How would *I* know?"

"Why did you take it to the police?"

"I didn't take it to the police. I couldn't even get it up out of the canal."

"You said the police have it."

I went through the whole thing for her, the complete play-by-play.

"I didn't tell them anything," I said. "What they know is only what they saw for themselves."

There were several moments of silence that were not quite silence. At the other end of the line Julie was mumbling. I wanted to think that she was mumbling to herself. I could make nothing of the words, but I was hoping it wasn't a low-voiced consultation with someone she had with her.

"I'm crazy to trust you," she said. "Steve wouldn't."

"Give me his number," I said. "I'll try him."

"No. It's better not. Can I borrow your Porsche?"

"Baby doesn't roll unless she has me on board," I said.

"Would you take me somewhere?"

"Like out of the country quick?" I asked.

"No," she said. "Just to where we were yesterday morning. Not where you picked us up, near there."

"The houses marked for demolition?"

"Yes. There."

"Why?"

"Nothing. It's just something I must see."

CHAPTER 4

I forgot that I was tired. I forgot about sleep. A girl can do that to a man. I can't say that I forgot about bed. That, after all, is something that a girl can't do for a man. I climbed into a pair of slacks, dragged a pullover down over my head, and stepped into a pair of loafers. Down at the hotel desk I fattened my wallet with a modest infusion of guilders. I grabbed a cab over to the garage.

Although it had to take the one-way-street circuitous route, at that hour on the edge of dawn traffic was negligible and it could zip around. So it was a few minutes quicker than walking the as-the-crow-flies route. Also, just that night in crow flight I had been chopped down. That may sound like a loss of nerve. I like to think that it was nothing more than the fact that I was on an errand that made me feel resistant to interruptions.

Pulling Baby out of the garage was quick. It hadn't been so much time since I'd put her in. They hadn't tucked her away. All the time I was asking myself why I should be pressing so much to jump through hoops for Julie Grant. She was lovely to look at. She could be sweet. It had been a fine evening, and I was concerned for her. I couldn't believe she wasn't in trouble.

On the other hand, I had asked questions. The answers she had given me amounted to little more than nothing. The answers, however, and the silences that punctuated them carried too many implications that put a tarnish on the evening's remembered pleasures.

Steve Dale had been thinking I was a spy. He'd pegged me for being CIA. The word that I had seen one of the plaster heads had been a shock to her. I couldn't have seen it because I had been with her. Her explanation that I couldn't have seen it without her having seen it too struck me as lame. I had come down with the unflattering thought that there had been a reason for this evening she and I had enjoyed together, and the reason wasn't that she had been overcome with an urge to take dinner with me. The reason, I had come to think, was that there had been something afoot and she had been assigned to keep the presumed spy well away from it.

I had been used and misused. Almost from the first I had been having my doubts about my misadventure at the footbridge. I had trouble with believing that I had merely fallen afoul of a simple footpad. The guy had been too simple. He had pulled off an event of conflicting dimensions. The violence of the assault had been disproportionately great. The size of the take had been disproportionately small. Also, there were those small panel trucks. I'd seen one in Dale's street. I'd seen one in Julie's street. In the shadow of one I'd been clunked.

It could well have been that the guilders had been lifted out of my wallet to set up a smoke screen around the real reason for clubbing me down. I had been searching my mind for the real reason, and now I was thinking that perhaps Julie had given it to me. It had been important that I shouldn't see the plaster head. Had it been that I had come up on the footbridge at just the wrong moment? Another step and I would have seen it?

I reminded myself that, in spite of everything, I did see

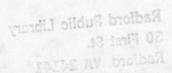

it. Thinking about that, I was telling myself it made no difference. The expectation had been that it wouldn't be there for me to see. Thrown into the canal, it would sink out of sight. A bundle of straw, of course, doesn't sink. It's much too light, but my phony footpad might not have known that, or in a moment of crisis he might have forgotten. There was only one certainty, and that was that I hadn't been clubbed by Archimedes.

There were other possibilities. He might have dumped the dummy under the bridge expecting that it wouldn't float out to where it could be seen. He hardly could have foreseen that, on coming to, I was going to drape myself over the bridge rail. Fastidious Erridge wouldn't just bend over and puke onto the pavement.

I had moved fast and in the predawn traffic lull Baby made the run over to Julie's place in next to no time at all. Julie, however, had also moved fast. When I came around the corner, she was there, dressed and out in the street waiting for me. She was also impatient. Before I could even come to a stop, she had her hand on the door handle and was pulling the car door open. She came aboard in a lightning jump and hauled the car door shut after her.

Like me, she had given the minimum time to dressing. We were something like a twin act. Slacks, pullovers, and loafers, and that was it. On me the absence of a bra under my sweater meant nothing. On her it meant a lot, far too much for a guy who had been planning on being firm with her, firm and stern and all that jazz.

I tried. "Don't you think it's time I was told what this is all about?" I asked.

I was thinking that I should have stopped at the curb and stayed stopped until I had some useful answers, but they look so small and worried and frightened. They melt a guy.

"It's nothing," she said. "It's really just a sort of joke."

"The sort that gets me knocked on the head. You'll tell me when I should start laughing."

"It was a sort of joke. Now I'm afraid it's gone sour."

"And the CIA can't be permitted to share in the laugh," I said.

"Are you or aren't you?" she asked.

"Am I what?"

"That's what I'm asking. What are you, Matt?"

"A sucker for little girls," I said. "In collision mat, in slinky dress, in sweater without a bra, they twist me around a little finger."

"I wish I could believe that," she said.

"How much evidence do you need?" I asked. "Here I am taking you where you want to go."

"That's just it. Are you taking me where I want to go, or are you using me to tell you where you'll find what you want?"

"If anybody's being used, baby, it's Erridge."

"Just because I asked you this little favor?"

"Just because we had an evening of me playing Don José to your Carmen," I said.

"What does that mean?"

"She kept him occupied with her blandishments while her smuggler buddies did their smuggling."

"Nobody did any smuggling."

"In the opera they did."

"You're being ridiculous."

"That's the pathos of us Don Josés. The Carmens make us ridiculous."

"You didn't enjoy our evening?"

"Don José enjoyed the blandishments, but when a man recognizes that there was nothing in it beyond his being used, the joy goes out of it."

"That's just not true," she said.

"What isn't?"

"It's not true that I was just using you. I like you, Matt. You're sweet. Whatever you are, you're sweet."

"CIA," I said. "Candied Intelligence Agent."

"You mean you are?"

"Sweet? Yes. CIA? No."

"Of course, you wouldn't tell me if you were. You couldn't. It's silly to ask."

"It's sillier to think it."

"You know Fredrik Dorstman. How would an ordinary American just passing through know Fredrik Dorstman?"

"I could think of ways, but there's no point in trying. I'm not an ordinary American just passing through. I am an American engineer sufficiently extraordinary to have been asked to Amsterdam to discuss the possibility of taking on a job that a lot of big Dutch money is itching to finance. That rubs me up against big-Dutch-money people and big-Dutch-money people associate with other big-Dutch-money people. That way I get to meet people I want to know, people I would just as soon not know, and people I don't give a damn about one way or the other."

"That's what you said. Dorstman was just another guest at a dinner you were asked to."

"The truth, the whole truth, and nothing but the truth. He was someone I didn't give a damn about one way or the other, perhaps with a little overlay of someone I would just as soon not know. I met him. I broke bread with him. I can't say I cottoned to him."

"It sounds reasonable," she said.

"It happens all the time," I said. "It's the social side of business. You get introduced to all kinds of people, including some you wouldn't want to touch with that well-known ten-foot pole. So what's with Dorstman that makes anybody who just happens to have met him automatically CIA?"

"He owns those houses. He's going to build the parking garage. He's going to build it unless he can be stopped."

"And the CIA is hooked on parking garages?"

"The CIA is into everything," she said. "Everything that hurts the poor and the helpless. Wherever people have been pushed too far and they rebel, the CIA is in there to put them down. You know that as well as I do. Everybody knows it."

Since it was just coming up daybreak, Baby was tooling along in fine fashion. She had the streets and the avenues pretty much to herself. There was some traffic, but almost all of it was going the other way, headed in toward the center. For the most part it was trucks. The milk and the produce were coming into the city.

We were coming up on that stretch of street to which she had asked me to take her. I'd had some answers—at least, answers of a sort. She hadn't denied the Don José–Carmen act. She had only denied that it had been the whole of it. Erridge was sweet. So what? So was Don José. Didn't Micaela say as much?

We came to the row of houses and I pulled up. I hadn't counted them when I had passed there before, but it hit me now. They were a row of six. They were old houses but not like the ones in the better parts of town where they had been well maintained through the centuries or, failing that, meticulously restored. These were old wrecks but, like the others, they were tall and narrow. They had the narrow doors and it was obvious that inside they would have the steep and narrow stairways. At the top of the facade of each of them there was that familiar Amsterdam hook ready for the hoisting of massive furniture in or out of windows.

The sun had come up while we were on the way. In full daylight it was no trouble seeing the use to which the six hooks had been put. It was gallows use. It was six hooks and six hangings—Fredrik Dorstman multiplied by six and hanged in effigy.

Julie gave them only a quick look before she turned on me. She was angry again. There was some confusion in it. She looked as though she didn't know whether to be worried or furious.

"You're going to a doctor," she said. "I should have known. I should have insisted."

"Known what?" I asked.

"Either you've been lying to me or you've been seeing things. You're going to a doctor. That way I'll know what you are, or you'll be getting the care you should be having."

"If I was seeing things, kid, so were two policemen. You're forgetting that, or will you get them to a doctor too?"

"Another of your lies. Steve did six heads for the effigies. You can see the six up there. So what did you see?"

"A seventh. He did a spare."

"He did six. There was no reason to do a spare. Steve hates doing duplicates. He's an artist. He's creative. He loathed repeating himself. He had to drive himself to do six."

"If you say so," I said. "How about someone else using the mold and making a seventh for some crazy purpose of his own?"

"That could be," she said.

Even though I'd suggested the possibility, I knew it couldn't be. I had seen the one I'd tried to rescue from the canal. It had been the worse for having been submerged, but the damage had not gone so far that I couldn't recognize the way the plaster had been painted. That much, even if nothing more, had been from Steve Dale's hand.

Hanging as they were high on the six facades, from where we were down at street level they weren't offering us any close-up view. Staring up at them, I began to notice something that had escaped me on first look. Dale had known what he was doing. His exaggerations of form in the modeling, accented by the further exaggerations of the painting, had not all been in the interest of savage grotesquery. He had made his heads with the specific intention that they should be visible and recognizable when seen from street level. He had taken into account the distance and the angle of vision.

What I first began to notice was that, although all six were swaying in the wind, one of the six consistently showed less of a response to wind pressure than did the other five. It seemed to me that this one dummy would be heavier than the others. Once that difference had drawn my attention to it, it hit me that there was also another difference. The head on that one seemed only a blob. Seen from street level, it didn't register with anything like the force of the other five.

I reached for the glove compartment. I remembered that I had a pair of binoculars in the glove compartment.

I had been over to Rotterdam to watch some yacht racing, and the glasses had been in the glove compartment ever since.

I brought them out. They're good glasses. They brought the heads in where they looked as though they were winding up to spit in my eye. That went for five of them. The sixth was something else again. Its face wasn't painted. It was generally ashen in color. Its mouth gaped open and the tongue protruded. I brought the glasses down.

"I don't think you want to look," I said. "There are five of Dale's heads up there. The sixth is not an effigy. The sixth is a real hanging."

She reached for the glasses.

"That's nonsense," she said. "He wouldn't."

"Are you sure you want to look?"

"You think I won't," she said. "You think I'll believe your stupid lie?"

I let her have the glasses.

"Okay," I said. "Third from the left."

She took the glasses and she studied the heads in turn. She started from the right. Whether the kid didn't know hay foot from straw foot or she thought that she would be showing me that she didn't take any stock in a word I said, I didn't know. I soon found out. She came to the third from the right and she brought down the glasses.

"You are a stupid liar," she said. "You thought I'd be afraid to look."

"If you aren't afraid to look," I said, "then you don't know left from right. You stopped one too soon. It's the next one, third from the left."

She brought the glasses back up to her eyes and looked. Just then I heard the sirens. They were sounding full blast and they were coming our way. She was kneeling on the car seat. I made a grab at her and hauled her down as I moved to gun the Porsche away from the curb. She tried to fight me, but sometime in there she became aware of the sirens and the fight went out of her.

For a few minutes neither of us was saying anything. I was completely occupied with Baby. She was moving us away fast, but I had to concentrate on the sirens, guiding on them to take us in directions for diminishing sound. All this speed was great, but not if it was going to serve only to hurry us into the arms of the police. Julie was using those same minutes for pulling herself out of shock. She was sitting wide-eyed beside me, huddled and shaking.

The siren sound came down to something faint and distant. Before it faded out completely, however, it bit off into silence. The cops had reached their destination. They had come to a halt at hangman's row. I brought Baby down to something less in excess of the legal speed limit, but I kept going. We couldn't put too much distance between ourselves and that demolition site and its gruesome embellishments. Julie was the first to speak.

"It isn't," she said.

"We can't kid ourselves, Julie. It is."

"I didn't have time really to see, but I was sure it wasn't," she said.

"I couldn't give you any more time," I said. "I don't know how far you are into this thing, but I want to think you aren't. I want to think I can keep you out of it."

She made no response to that. Maybe she was choosing to give me nothing, but I don't think it was that. Just then she was having a concern that took precedence over everything else. She repeated what she had first said, but now she was making it a question.

"It isn't," she said. "You had a long look. Tell me."

"It's a dead body," I said. "Five hangings in effigy and one real hanging."

"I know. I saw that."

"Then you know. Why do you keep asking?"

"Not that," she said. "Is it him?"

"Who?"

"Fredrik Dorstman."

"No. At that distance and in that condition, whoever it is isn't at his most recognizable, but it isn't Dorstman. Dorstman is shorter, fatter, and older."

"Then who?"

Automatically I would have asked her how she could have expected me to know. Although the question did pass through my mind, I shoved it aside. In the role for which they had me cast, the CIA spy, it would have been inevitable that I should have been expected to know. More than that, however, I came down with the notion that she wanted me to tell her that the hanged man wasn't Steve Dale.

I gave that possibility some hard thought. Height and bulk ruled Fredrik Dorstman out, but on the view I'd had of the dead man any subtler distinction was difficult if not impossible to make. If I was right about the focus of her concern, however, I thought of something that gave me a possible answer.

"Unless he cut his hair and shaved off his beard," I said, "it isn't Steve. I saw that much—burr cut and clean shaven."

"I knew it wasn't Steve," she said.

"You got to see that much?"

"I never even thought of it. I know where Steve is."

"Where?"

"Where I left him, in my place."

I could think of nothing she could have said that I would have liked less. Am I sounding like a blue-nosed Puritan? I promise you it wasn't that. Green-eyed might have been closer to the mark, but you must consider my feeling in the context of the evening she and I had had together.

That she had gone straight from sleeping against my shoulder to sleeping with another guy—there's a thought that would sour any man. I was remembering that moment on the phone when I hadn't known whether she had taken to mumbling to herself or she was conferring with someone before coming back on the line to me. I was thinking that now I knew which it had been.

I thought I was taking it with stoical self-control. I was saying nothing of what I was thinking, but my face must have given me away.

"It isn't what you think," she said. "Not that it matters, but it isn't."

"It doesn't matter," I said.

"It does to you. I can see it does."

"It's all right," I said. "I'm not going to kill you. That much Don José I am not."

"Oh, stop it," she said. "We're not in a silly opera."

"We're in a silly something, and it's time you told me what."

"After I talked to you," she said, "and before I started dressing, I made a quick call to Steve and told him what you'd said. We knew something had gone wrong and I wanted him to get away from the studio as quickly as possible. I told him to come to my place and stay there till we found out."

She explained that she had wanted to think that I had

been knocked on the head and had hallucinated, that I had seen nothing and that there was nothing to worry about.

"I was trying very hard to think that," she said. "Not that I was wishing you a concussion or anything like that. I hope you can believe that, because it is the honest truth."

"I'm trying to believe it," I said.

"Anyhow, even though it was my first thought," she said, "I couldn't make it stand up to any second thinking. There was the one thing that made it too unlikely."

"What thing?" I asked.

She explained. I had seen the six plaster heads on the studio table. They had made a strong impression on me. That I should have hallucinated seeing one of them again was all too possible, but that hadn't been all of what I'd told her I'd seen. I'd seen it attached to a straw dummy dressed in old clothes.

"I could see no way that you could have hallucinated all of that," she said. "You didn't see the dummies when you were in the studio. That left only two possibilities."

She outlined the two possibilities for me. One was that I had seen a dummy or the six of them elsewhere and that, therefore, I was the spy Dale thought I was and their thing had gone wrong because I knew too much. The other was that I was telling the truth and then, even though I wasn't a spy, things had gone seriously wrong anyhow.

"The dummy couldn't have been in the canal," she said. "That was no part of the program. It had to be that someone was getting into the act and the whole thing had gone out of control."

"Okay," I said. "That brings us back to the question I've been asking all along. What was the program?"

She squirmed. She wanted to tell me and she didn't want to tell me.

"If I knew I could trust you," she said.

"Carmen never doubted that she could trust Don José, and she never had any reason to doubt," I said.

"This isn't Bizet."

"No, it's bizarre. Anyhow, Bizet just did the music. The story was Mérimée's."

"I couldn't care less. I wish you'd drop it."

"Trust me and I'll drop it," I promised.

"Publicity," she said.

The demonstration of the previous morning had been given a good play on the television news. The plan had been to build on that beginning. The six effigies hanging on the six facades were to be great stuff for newspaper pictures and for TV coverage. Anonymous tips had gone out to the papers and the TV people. Dorstman was to become a household word. They had expected that he would be able to go nowhere without being faced with derision and contempt.

"People have to have it driven home to them what this horrible man is doing," she said. "The opposition of a lot of rebellious kids isn't enough. That won't stop him. It will take a wave of popular revulsion. The people who have homes, the people who are living in comfort, have to be drawn into it. Maybe they wouldn't have any effect on Dorstman. He might ignore them and go ahead, but the government wouldn't be able to ignore them. People must have it called to their attention, and it must be kept before their eyes because people are likely to forget. Trade union people and even the middle class. There are a lot of middle-class people who have hearts. They wouldn't be able to sleep in their comfortable beds at night if it could be kept constantly before them that there are people who have no place to lay their heads."

"And that's all?" I asked.

"That's all."

"Then why did you have to get Dale out of the studio? What's he got to hide from?"

"That body up there," she said. "That was murder, wasn't it?"

"It sure looked like it, but before we went down there and saw the body, murder never entered my mind. How come you thought of it?"

"I didn't."

"But you lost no time about getting Dale out of the studio and hidden away in your place. Why? What were you afraid of?"

"I didn't know."

She didn't know but she did have ideas. Some of them had been crazy and some not so crazy, or at least that was the way they seemed to me. There had been, of course, the ideas she'd been having about me. Whether they had been planted in her thinking by Steve Dale or whether she'd been having them on her own made little difference. She'd been having them. She spelled them out for me.

It came back to CIA Dirty Trickster Erridge. Wasn't it common knowledge that there was no deed so foul that the CIA wouldn't stoop to it? She had been unable to imagine what I might have been doing, but she hadn't been able to escape the thought that it could have been something to put Steve Dale into deep trouble.

"You must admit," she said, "that what has been done, horrible as it is, will serve their purpose. Oh, yes. It will serve it only too well. Popular revulsion? Where is it going to go now? It's going to go against Steve and the rest of the kids. People will think they're murderers."

"Somebody's a murderer," I said.

"Not Steve."

"How do you know? He had me out of the way, but he also had you out of the way. What do you know about how he spent the night?"

"That's a horrible thing to say about him."

"And not a horrible thing to say about me?"

"You could be under orders. I know Steve isn't."

"You really believe that of me?"

"No," she said. "I can't. Things keep coming up that should make me believe it, but then I can't. So I always end up the same way. I don't know and I wish I did."

"Steve," I said, "hasn't been in this alone. What about the other people?"

She moaned.

"Yes," she said.

"Yes, what?"

Just as she didn't know what she was to believe about me, she didn't know what she was to believe about Dale's partners in protest. Theirs was the standard picture. They were completely united on the ends; on means they had differences. Steve Dale belonged to the passive-resistance faction. They would demonstrate. They would have their heads broken. They would never take an aggressive position. They would never fight back. Their weapons would be martyrdom and derision.

There were others who itched for violence. The tamer of those urged more positive action but it was no more than nuisance action, like tossing stink bombs into police stations. There were, however, still others who were of a more savage persuasion. They pushed for things like a few sticks of dynamite wired to the ignition of Fredrik Dorstman's Mercedes.

"When I saw that body up there," Julie said, "I thought they had done it. The bomb in his car would just have killed him. Doing it this way they would put it on to Steve."

"But it isn't Dorstman," I reminded her.

"I don't think that makes much difference," she said.

"To Dorstman it makes a lot of difference."

She dismissed that as being beside the point. Lining a murder victim up among his effigies, whoever the murder victim, was still putting it on to Steve Dale.

"You are thinking that there are people or even one person," I said, "who at the cost of wrecking their protest would commit a murder for no reason but to make things tough for Dale?"

"Not as simple as that," she said. "I think there are some crazy enough to think that a real hanging will be even stronger publicity."

"Murder just for publicity? Come on!"

"Bombing a police station would kill policemen. That body—maybe it's a policeman."

"Their fight isn't with the police. It's with Fredrik Dorstman," I said.

"The police are on his side. You saw what happened yesterday morning. You saw what they did to Steve."

"And somebody gets even for Steve's busted head," I said, "and chooses to do it in a way that will make Steve a suspect. Even for the craziest of your friends that's a bit too screwy."

"Steve wasn't the only one who got a busted head yesterday morning," she said.

CHAPTER 5

She was thinking aloud. It was tangled thinking and, even as she talked, she kept trying to unsnarl it. She built a picture that had one or more of the violent ones, while pretending to go along on Dale's effigy hangings, sneaking back to take over with a hanging of their own. Convinced that a killing was needed to punch their message home, they would think that just a simple murder wouldn't do it. That could go down as just another act of violence in a too violent world. They could phone the papers with anonymous calls to claim the killing for their group of protesters, and they might or might not be believed. Hanging the body in Steve's row of effigies would deliver not only a far stronger message. It would amount to a signed message.

"What they might be doing to Steve," she said, "wouldn't even enter their heads. Anyhow, even if they did think of that, it wouldn't bother them too much. After all, Steve is an American."

"Americans are fair game, even if the American is a buddy giving his all for your good cause?" I asked.

It wasn't as simple as that. In the kid's tangled thinking nothing was simple. Steve was an American and Steve was rich. The popular thinking has it that rich Americans can get away with anything anywhere.

"They'd be thinking that Steve was the one who could

take it," she said. "He'd just be put out of the country or he'd buy his way out or something. It's the way they think. I know them. Foreigners all have those ideas about us. Then there's the other thing."

"There's always the other thing, Julie," I said. "What's it now?"

"They're paranoid. Everywhere they look, they see CIA."

If there has ever been a place for the old line about the pot calling the kettle black, this was it. What she was saying, however, was too provocative. I was saying nothing to turn her away from pursuing it further.

"Their good buddy, Steve Dale?" I asked.

"It's like a disease," she said. "It's infectious. Everybody is suspicious and everybody is suspect. If one of them did it and it wasn't a policeman that was murdered, it will be one of their own who they found was a spy or they just suspected of spying."

"The way you see them," I said, "they're walking around wanting to be betrayed. They're so set on expecting it that without it they don't feel authentic."

"That's it," she said. "As for Steve, I'm sure there are some of them who simply can't believe that an American who has everything going for him can really be one of them. That's part of the reason why Steve had to be in the front of it yesterday and get his silly head broken. He's always trying to prove himself to them."

"So apart from what you thought about me," I asked, "this is what had you frightened for Dale?"

"I've been frightened for him all along," she said. "I couldn't imagine anything like murder, but if you were telling the truth and you had been hit on the head and all that, then I knew that much. One of them was being violent and he was mixing up his violence with Steve's effigies. Why wouldn't I be frightened?"

"I'd think the shoe should be on the other foot," I said. "Steve's sticking his neck out for them and out of what—the goodness of his heart? Shouldn't they be proving themselves to him?"

"*You* think so," she said, "and *I* think so. I've told Steve as much, but he just won't see it. He says they're right not to trust him. It's like he doesn't quite trust himself. He keeps saying that he's middle-class and that the middle class is rotten. He says he knows that and they know it. It comes down to his hating himself for being what he calls middle-class, and he works overtime at not being it."

Since she was agreeing with me, there wasn't much I could say to that. I dropped it. By that time we were back in familiar territory, skirting the canals.

"Where do I take you?" I asked.

"Home, please."

"To Steve?"

"I have to tell him what happened. The police will be coming after him."

"They'll know? You expect his good buddies will finger him?"

"Someone already has. It's not as though all the effigies were taken away. Only the one was taken away, and the idea must have been to make it disappear so that it would look as though Steve had done only five effigies and had left room for the one hanging. Five of the effigies were left hanging and they'll lead the police to Steve."

"Connoisseur cops who'll recognize the Dale style?" I asked.

"He's the only sculptor in the movement and he hasn't been keeping himself inconspicuous."

"Will they know about you?" I asked.

"How can you tell what they know? I'm going to have to get Steve out of the country, but first I'll have to talk him into going. He's so crazy stubborn."

"Can I help?"

"Do you want to?"

"This is trouble," I said, "and you won't do anything to keep yourself out of it. I want to keep you clear of it."

"I'll be all right," she said.

"Who's crazy stubborn now?"

She preferred not to answer that one.

"It won't be easy to get Steve to trust you," she said.

"Because he has me tagged for something worse than middle-class?"

"Because you know Dorstman."

I put a hand up to my head bandage. "Steve Dale and I," I said, "both have one of these. Won't that make us brothers or something?"

"You weren't clubbed by the police."

"Okay. For Steve Dale the police are the enemy, but they aren't all of the enemy. There's Fredrik Dorstman, and now there's somebody who's doing Steve dirt. Since this somebody is obviously the same somebody who knocked me on the head, is he going to be so stubborn that he won't see that there's now a bond between us? In his assortment of enemies he and I seem to be sharing one."

"If he believes you," she said.

"That goes two ways. I'll have to believe him."

She grabbed at that. "You'll get him out of the country?" she said.

"If he can convince me that he isn't a murderer."

To that she responded with airy assurance.

"Oh, that," she said. "I know Steve. You can take my word for it. He never could do it. It isn't in him."

"Not even to prove himself?"

"Prove himself? How?"

"By demonstrating his complete lack of middle-class morality. You know. If it's for the cause, it isn't murder. It's war."

"He doesn't accept that. He never has and he never will. He's a pacifist. He says war is murder. I know him. Also, how can you say it's for the cause? It's ruined everything."

I pulled up in front of her place. I more than half expected that I would be dismissed at the street door, and I had come to no decision about how I would handle that. I had been thinking that I might force my way in. I had also thought that I might present an ultimatum. She wasn't going in unless I went in with her. I had pictures of wrestling her away from the door.

I got out of the car. She sat tight till I had come around and opened the car door for her. Even then she didn't move. I could guess that she was thinking about what she was to do next.

"You're home, Julie," I said.

"I know."

She was slow coming out of the car and slow going across the pavement to her door, slow bringing out her latchkey.

"Changing your mind?" I asked. "Don't want to go in?"

I was hoping she would say yes even though I could find no way of sucking myself into expecting it. Without replying she opened the door and she made no move to close it in my face. Once inside, however, she stopped.

"I think," she said, "it will be better if I go up alone. I'll have to explain my bringing you here, prepare him."

I could see no way that it would be better.

"If," I said, "it's to give him time to get his pants on, don't let that worry you. It won't worry me."

That drew me a look of contempt, but she started upstairs and made no objection to my following her. She was letting me know that my line didn't merit a reply. She was going to prove something. She opened the door of her apartment. While it wasn't any such big spread as Dale had, it wasn't the humble pad of any impoverished student either. The kid did pretty well. There was luxury in evidence.

The door opened directly on a large living room, but for the population it contained it was no larger than it needed to be. It wasn't crowded but it was well filled. Steve was there but he wasn't alone. They were all over the place, draped along the sofa, sprawled in chairs, sitting cross-legged on the floor. Steve Dale's and mine weren't the only heads wrapped in surgical gauze. There were a couple more. Apart from Dale there was only one of the company I had ever seen before. That was Piet Claes.

They were a scruffy-looking lot. The only neat touches to be seen on any of them were the head bandages. Not the one I had done for Dale, but the others. Those looked like mine—professional.

Scruffy, however, was all of it. They didn't look underfed. They were a brawny lot with good outdoorsman color. Apart from that, they did look what in the language of the day would be called disadvantaged. You know those random thoughts that will come trooping through your mind. At that hardly appropriate moment I had one.

I was thinking that there's nothing better than a picket line for getting kids out into the fresh air.

It was inappropriate thinking for that moment, because I was standing in the doorway confronted with mass hostility. Dale spoke for the company. His scowl was for me, but his words were for Julie.

"Did you have to bring him here?"

"He's all right," Julie said. "He'll help. He wants to help."

"In a pig's eye," Steve said.

He was speaking through a general rumbling. Such of it as was in Dutch I could only guess at from its tone. I hadn't the first doubt, however, but that I was making good guesses. Part of the rumble was in French and part in German. Some of it was even in English. All of those were close equivalents to Dale's "pig's eye."

"It's trouble," Julie said. "Bad trouble, a lot worse than you can think."

"He's trouble," Dale said.

"You can be facing a murder rap, my friend."

Someone had to say something if the conversation was ever to come unstuck. I thought that was going to do it, but getting an *idée fixe* unfixed is rarely easy.

"Who's going to pin it on me?" Dale asked. "You? Also, I'd like it better if you cut the 'friend' crap."

I turned to Julie. "Tell them," I said.

"He wasn't lying," she said. "One of them was in the canal. He did see it there. He was clubbed unconscious and, when he came to, he saw it. Look at his head."

"Anybody can wrap himself in a bandage," Dale said. "Who knows whether he's got anything under it?"

"I've got a brain under it," I said. "I'm wondering what you have under yours."

Julie pushed back into it. "If you will just listen," she said. "It was where he said it was in the canal. It was there because there are only five still hanging, or there *were* five. The police must have them by now. The sixth wasn't the effigy. It was a real hanging, a real corpse, and whoever, whatever, or whyever, they'll be calling it murder."

Certainly that should have rocked them back, but it didn't. They simply didn't believe her.

"That what he's been telling you?" Dale said.

The others were talking all at once. The bits of the general babble that came in languages I could handle were all taking the same line. Nobody could tell them. They knew. They had done the hanging of the six effigies and nobody could tell them that they didn't know what they had hoisted up onto the hooks.

Julie persisted. "That's it," she said. "You put up all six, and then somebody came along and took one of them down to put the real hanging in its place."

I finished it for her. "And then took the dummy he'd replaced and hauled it back to this part of town to dump it in the canal," I said.

It was Claes who picked up on that.

"That's crazy," he said. "Why would anyone do that? Haul it halfway across the city instead of just dumping it out there?"

"The whole story is crazy," Dale said.

"Crazy or not, I saw it with my own eyes," Julie told him. "Five effigies hanging in a row and in the middle of them a sixth, a dead man hanging up there with them."

Everyone was saying crazy and I was thinking crazy, but I was looking at a huge drawing laid out on Julie's worktable. It was a big table, nothing the size of the one

Dale had in his studio, but far from small. He had pushed her books and notes to one side and he had almost the whole of the tabletop covered with the great sheet of paper on which he had done the drawing.

It was a poster. Size and style were telling me that. It was the grotesque of Dorstman again, but now he was portrayed in the performance on a motor car of an act that was none the less obscene for being impossible. Steve Dale's genius was wide-ranging. The guy could do pornography with the masters.

The first break in their massed incredulity came from the German. The others called him Kraky. As the thing went on, I picked up on their names. He was Heinrich Krakenbaum. Later, when Julie gave me a fill-in on the various individuals, he was on her list of the ones with an itch for violent action. She was ready to swear that he had never engaged in any, but she was equally certain that he was ambitious to begin.

"*Aber wer?*" he asked.

Since he wanted to know, he might have been ready to listen and to believe.

"*Wer hat es getan oder wer ist gestorben?*" I asked.

He answered me. He wasn't expecting me to tell him the name of the hangman. He was asking who had been hanged. I explained that, as a stranger in town, I knew only a very few people in Amsterdam. I'd had a good long look at the dead man, but it had been at a distance and from a difficult angle. Even with glasses it had been difficult. In any case, the fact that it had been nobody I recognized meant nothing. It wasn't likely that it would have been a face that I'd know.

Since some of the others were now looking blank and

they had been able to follow when we'd been doing it in English, I switched out of the German.

"Julie got only a very quick look," I said, "before we heard the police sirens and I had to get her away from there before the cops arrived."

The one crack in their unanimity was enough. It spread quickly. They all came around to accepting the incredible.

"Anyone you recognized?" Dale put the question to Julie.

The kid shuddered. "He looked horrible," she said. "Dead people look so different and dead the way he was with his face horribly contorted and on just the quickest look through the glasses, even if it was someone I knew . . ."

"But it wasn't?"

It was the Frenchman who asked that. The others seemed to be making the inference, but that's the French of it. He had to have it pinned down. His name was René Blanc, which must have been the reason why they called him Whitey. Julie was ready to go all out in classifying him as nonviolent. She said he was the complete intellectual. I wasn't so sure that it followed. Complete intellectuals with a compulsion to prove their manhood have been known to outsavage the savages.

"I don't think it was," Julie said. "It's so hard to say."

The one I had spotted as English was the quickest to understand and the quickest to sympathize.

"Back home," he said, "I've seen a lot of dead and even some that died by hanging. Even wives can have trouble recognizing them. Sometimes they do it only by the clothes."

Of course, he wasn't English. He was Irish. His name

was Sean O'Hare. Julie was fond of the guy. He had the Irish good looks and more than his share of the Irish charm. When I later questioned her about him, it was only with the greatest reluctance that she put him among the violent ones.

"You know how the Irish are," she said, "always talking big. When you get to know him, he's sweet."

There were three more of them and, including Piet Claes, they were all three Amsterdam natives. I've told you that, besides Dale and myself, two of the others had bandaged heads. O'Hare was one, and the other was a Dutch kid, Jan Maes. The third Dutchman and Claes Julie had tagged for being cream puffs, but Jan was violent. He had a well-established record for it. Just on the look of him, however, I'd had him written off from the first.

He looked stupid enough for it, but that was all. Although in size he was a match for the biggest of them, where on the others it was good hard muscle, on him it was blubber. He bulged with fat. I could believe he was mean enough. You don't find them meaner than the mean fat man, but I'm an engineer.

Though I've never had any part in a hanging, I have an engineer's exact appreciation of just what it takes to raise a weight. I could imagine Jan Maes exerting as much power as it might take to squeeze a trigger or to toss a small bomb. Call it a pint-size Molotov cocktail, but he just didn't have what it would take for pulling off a hanging.

Piet Claes was the first to give it a practical turn. He spoke to Dale.

"You can't go back to the studio," he said, "and you can't stay here."

O'Hare was right in there with the Irish charm or, if you like, the Irish impudence.

"Yes, he can," he said. "Julie can come and live with me."

Julie scowled at him, but Claes was keeping it practical.

"He can't stay here," he said, "because of the police. When they don't find him at the studio, this will be the first place they'll look."

"So they'll look," Dale said. "Even the dumbest cop isn't going to believe that I'd louse up my own show."

"What they'll believe or not believe has nothing to do with it," Claes argued. "You can be sure they've got dossiers on all of us. They run through their files and they come up with *you*. It's too easy. You're the sculptor."

"What does that prove except that I'm the last man to do it?"

"It doesn't have to prove anything," Claes said. "You're the obvious one for them to pull in, and don't think they won't do it. They'll pull you in and they'll work you over."

Dale squared his shoulders and stuck his chin out. I could see the light of martyrdom come up in his eyes. Julie wasn't missing it.

"Listen to him, Steve," she said. "He's talking sense."

"So they'll work me over," Dale said. "They don't scare me."

"All right, man," Claes said. "You're brave. If you want to be brave for yourself, that's crazy; but you're going to be brave for the rest of us, and that's wrong."

"It'll be me," Dale said. "Why the rest of you?"

"They'll break you. You'll give them names."

Dale didn't like it. "You ought to know me better than that," he said.

"I know them better. You'll break. Everybody does. You won't want to, but you will. We all know you're a good man. They won't have an easy time with you, but if it can't be easy they know how to make it as hard as it has to be. Don't be a fool, Steve. You have to get away from here. We have to get you away."

"Listen to him, Steve," Julie was begging.

Claes turned to the others. "We're all in this together," he said. "We should all have a say. What about it? We get him out of the country and quick."

"How do we do that?" The question came from blubbery Jan Maes.

Nobody had an answer, but it was evident that Julie and Claes thought they might have one. Both of them looked at me expectantly. I knew what they were thinking. Baby was waiting down below at the curb, and Julie knew it. Claes may not have known that I had her that handy, but he could have been making a good guess. They knew that I had run Julie over to hangman's row and then brought her back home. Holland is a small country with good roads. The Porsche could make it to one border or another in quick time, and who would think to stop a Porsche? Isn't it a well-known fact that Porsches belong to middle-class establishment types? Porsches don't carry friends of the poor and the dispossessed.

I had known that this would be coming. Not from Piet Claes, of course, since I couldn't have known that, but it had been obvious from the start that it would be coming from Julie. I was seeing it as the only reason why she had allowed me to come up to the apartment with her. All along it had been at the back of my mind, trying to decide whether or not I would do it. Now that the moment had come, I discovered that I had decided.

Steve Dale had me convinced. The guy was an artist. What he made with his hands was the major event in his life. The hanging of the six effigies had been for the cause, but for Steve Dale it had been a great deal more than that. It had been his art exhibition. It had been an artist's happening. I mightn't have been able to answer for him on anything else, but of this one thing I was certain. The guy had created something. It was simply inconceivable that he should have had any part in lousing it up.

So if I was saying nothing, it was only because I was taking a moment or two to think out the strategy. In Holland the available borders are the Belgian and the German. I no sooner had thought of Belgium than I rejected it. Even though Benelux had always sounded to me like something an anxious housewife might use if she wants to have the whitest wash on the block, the three countries are locked in all sorts of close cooperation. Such cooperation might all too easily include the quick booting of a fugitive back across the border.

It would have to be Germany for that reason, even though I couldn't see that as the happiest of choices. The Germans had been having too much trouble of their own with the violently rebellious young. I could think of no country that would be warmly welcoming, but the situation, I felt, called for a place that might be more relaxed about it. I was thinking that the best bet would be east into Germany and then straight on through into Denmark.

I was lining up the routes in my head. It would be the E9 past Utrecht, then east on the E36 to follow the north bank of the Rhine to cross the border near Arnhem. In Germany I would bypass Duisberg, Essen, and Dortmund to hit the E3 for main highway all along by Bremen,

Hamburg, and Kiel for the Flensburg crossing into Denmark.

I came out of it to hear what Dale was saying.

"Forget it," he said. "I'm not running."

"If we take off right away," I told him, "I should be able to get you out. I'm thinking we can go east over the German border and on into Denmark. That'll be your best bet."

"With you?" he said. "Thank you very much, but no."

He had sold me on him, but he hadn't sold himself on me.

"Steve," Julie said. "Don't be a stubborn fool. You're wrong about Matt. I know you're wrong."

"If you know so much, you go with him. That I'm not running into any traps is the least of it. I'm simply not running." He turned away from her to talk to his buddies. "If you guys think you can't trust me not to give you away, then go find yourselves someplace to hide."

He picked the poster off the table and carefully rolled it up. With it he started for the door. Julie grabbed at his arm. He moved to shake her off but, thinking better of it, he stood.

"Where are you going with that?" she asked.

"Over to the Stedelijk, where I'm going to paste it to the wall," he said. "Then I'm going back to the studio."

"Steve, please," Julie said.

"Steve, that's asking for it," Claes said.

"Leave the man alone," O'Hare told them. "The man has guts. A man does what he has to do. I'm going with him, or better still . . ." He turned to Dale. "Let me have it, Steve. I'll go and paste it up for you."

"No," Dale said. "No, Sean. I'm doing this myself."

"You're not." Julie was still hanging on to his arm. "If you go, I'm going with you."

It was a nice bit of female strategy. She was thinking it would be a way to stop him. I was expecting it would work but it didn't. Either he was too much bent on martyrdom or he was pursuing strategies of his own. If only the guilty run when no man pursueth, it can be that only the innocent go rushing toward the pursuit.

"You'll be in the way," he said.

"I mean to be," Julie told him.

"You're a big girl," he said.

He went out the door and she went with him, still keeping her hold on his arm. I followed after them. I suppose I was thinking that he might find some way to push her off. I wanted to be there to catch her when he pushed. Out in the street he stopped a moment, looking at Baby and grinning.

"Like to run me over to the Stedelijk?" he said.

I suppose I should fill you in on the Stedelijk. It's Amsterdam's museum of modern art, as modern as the year after next. There it was again. In making his choice of where he would put up his poster, he was making the artist's choice.

"My offer still stands," I said. "Across into Germany and on into Denmark. Copenhagen's a great market for pornography."

Gently but firmly he detached Julie's hand from its grasp on his arm.

"Back upstairs," he said, "or, if you like, with him."

"I'm a big girl," she said.

He turned and started off. She followed right behind him. After a step or two he stopped and turned.

"Two strides behind me like a Chinese wife?" he asked.

"Like a Chinese wife," she said, "if you won't have me at your side."

He put his arm around her. "I'll have you at my side," he said.

He kissed her and they walked away from me together.

"That's it, Erridge," I told myself. "You're the face on the cutting-room floor. For you it's an episode closed."

I could tell myself that, but I wasn't quite ready to close it. She was little. She was sweet. She was gutsy, but she was also vulnerable. They walked down to that small panel truck that was again parked where I had seen it the day before. They got in and took off.

I climbed aboard the Porsche. Driving her around to the Stedelijk, I pulled up there. I was there when they came rolling up. No truck can outrun Baby. I stayed in the car and watched.

He unrolled his poster and stuck it up on the wall of the museum building. People on their way into the museum stopped to look. Just in the moments it took him to fix it to the wall a small crowd gathered. Stepping back from it, he took Julie's arm and with all the strut of a grand cavalier he piloted her through the semicircle of his audience. As they walked away, a ripple of laughter was running through the crowd. A few voices were raised in indignation. One woman darted forward and raised her hand to rip the poster from the wall. Two men came after her and pulled her away. The crowd, which had grown bigger, applauded.

Dale's fixing the poster to the museum wall was, of course, the main event, but there was something else that caught my attention as well. During those few minutes they had been away from the truck, it had been standing unlocked and with the key in the ignition. That could have been deliberate in preparation for a quick getaway or it could have been his customary procedure. A truck, I was telling myself, is a motor vehicle and, as Dale had said, motor vehicles aren't people. They are only things and Dale had a contempt for things.

Suddenly I was feeling bone-tired and shaky. To that moment I had forgotten that I had gone the whole night without sleep and the whole morning without breakfast. I looked at the dashboard clock and amended that to without breakfast and lunch. I set Baby rolling. I was asking myself if I was really interested in food. Sleep seemed to be taking precedence. All the way to the garage I was thinking of bed. I could have something up on room service, but I had doubts of staying awake long enough to get it eaten.

One of the boys in the garage was taking off for lunch. He offered me a lift to my hotel. I welcomed that, and all through the short ride I was working hard at not falling asleep. He was chatting and I was trying to be polite, even though I knew he was only practicing his English. He dropped me at the hotel entrance. As I went in, I was not much short of sleepwalking.

How many steps I took in the lobby with the two men walking with me, one at one arm and the second at the other, I don't know. I only gradually became aware of someone talking to me. I have a feeling that he had spoken several times before it came through to me.

"Mr. Erridge," he was saying. "I must ask you to come along with us."

I blinked and I looked at them, first the one and then the other. The man who was talking to me was nobody I knew. I recognized the other one. He was one of the two police officers who had hauled me up out of the canal.

CHAPTER 6

I should have kept my mouth shut, but if I was thinking at all I was thinking of bed. Since I was on my feet and I was seeing and hearing and speaking, you can say I was awake, but it was only technically. The rest of me had shut down.

"Could I see you later?" I said. "Right now I need sleep."

"You haven't been to bed all night, Mr. Erridge?"

"That's it and it's catching up with me."

"We'll want to know what you've been doing."

I can't say that I woke up, but I did become sufficiently awake to go wary. The police wanted to know what I'd been doing. I should have been making carefully considered decisions about that. Did I want to tell them anything and, if anything, how much? I suppose my decision-making apparatus wasn't completely turned off. It was just not geared up to giving anything careful consideration. I came to an unconsidered determination. I wasn't going to tell them anything.

"Give me two or three hours," I said. "More, if possible, but two or three hours. I'll need at least that much sleep before I can be any good to you."

"We won't keep you long, and then you can have all the sleep you want."

They had now taken me by the arms and were starting to guide me back out to the street. I tried hanging back.

"You'll have to tell me what this is about," I said.

"We are expecting *you* to tell *us*."

I thought of just walking out from between them and going up to bed, but that would have involved argument and possibly even a tussle. I hadn't the energy for either. They wanted me to come along. It seemed stupid of them to be wanting it. Surely they could see that I wouldn't be good for much. In retrospect I can believe that they might have been liking me the way I was, anything but alert.

I suppose I was sleepy enough to be apathetic. I was up to nothing but following the line of least resistance. I was even docile, but it wasn't Matt Erridge who was permitting himself to be escorted out to the police car. It was a zombie. The car was waiting at the curb with a cop behind the wheel. The lad I knew from the canal climbed into the back seat. I was helped in after him, and the guy in command came aboard to flank me on the other side.

It was a short ride and, in the course of it, he put some questions to me. He wanted a full account of my movements through the night and the morning. It seems to me that I got as far as saying I had taken a lady out to dinner. I also named the restaurant. I may have said more than that, but I think not. The next I knew I was being shaken awake. I had done the greater part of the ride asleep on my inquisitor's shoulder.

When we left the car, I had them on either side of me and they had me by the arms. They couldn't have been worrying about any chance that I might cut and run. If anything, they were supporting me as I stumbled along. We went into a building I didn't know, but then I was not in a state where I was knowing anything much.

Inside it was icy air and an acrid smell that put enough

bite on my nostrils to pull me at least partway out of my stupor. I was in a room that looked like a safe-deposit vault with outsize lockers. The penetrating chill almost immediately moved me away from that comparison. It was more like one of those places where people rent freezer space.

There was an attendant. One of my escorts spoke to him. I tried to put my mind on what the guy was saying. It was in Dutch, but I caught it because it was a number. That much Dutch I knew. Since it was only a number, however, I lost interest in it. The attendant went to one of the lockers and pulled it open. It came out like a drawer without sides, just a slab behind a drawer front. There was a body lying on the slab. It was an ugly sight. All of it was ugly, but the nastiest bit was the neck.

It was the body of a man. Around the neck there was a thin line that looked almost like a cut. It was set neatly at the center of a broader band of bruised flesh.

"I want you to look at this body," the man said.

I was looking. Something seemed to be expected of me.

"I see him," I said.

"Who is he?"

"Nobody I know."

"You've seen him."

I was ready to believe that I had, but it was only a conclusion I was pulling out of the mush that I then had serving me as a mind. The fact that they were showing him to me, combined with the marks on the dead man's neck, told me just what corpse it would be. So far as recognition went, however, I would have registered just as much on the body of any other man they might have pulled out of their lockers. I was just alert enough to keep all of that to myself.

"Not to remember," I said. "Somewhere on the street in passing perhaps, but then he wouldn't have been looking like this. Anyhow, I don't know him."

"On the street," the man said.

He added the name of the street and pinned it down between the cross streets. He was right on the nose for hangman's row.

"He's nobody I know," I said.

"Apart from just seeing him on the street?"

"If I saw him at all," I said.

They took me out of there. My teeth were chattering and I was turning blue. I hadn't dressed for cold storage and they had me at a time when my vitality was at low ebb. Tucked back in the car between my two companions I warmed up. With warmth sleep came back over me. It was again a short ride, but I know that only because both rides were repeated later when I was awake and aware. This time I slept all the way, and again I had to be shaken awake and led stumbling out of the police car.

At this second stop I was taken into a warm room. It was more than warm. It was too warm. It had the smell that goes with police stations the world over—a whiff of varnish, a whiff of disinfectant, a whiff of sweat, and more than a whiff of dust. Again they had something for me to look at and again it was bodies, six of them. These, however, weren't real bodies. They were Steve Dale's six effigies.

"You recognize these," the man said.

I zeroed in on the water-damaged one.

"This one," I said. I turned to the other cop. "You helped me get this one up out of the canal last night."

I was being the helpful type, refreshing the cop's memory for him.

"The other five?"

That was the inquisitor. The cop was saying nothing.

"They weren't in the canal," I said. I had to stop long enough to get past a yawn. It was the kind of yawn that threatens to unhinge your jaws. "You can see they haven't been in the water."

I wasn't looking at the six dummies anymore. I couldn't because my eyes were closing. A stupid cop could have taken it for evasive action, but the inquisitor wasn't stupid. He knew exhaustion when he saw it. He may have tried to question me some more, but if he did I've wiped it out.

The wipeout was complete. I slept. It was the best kind of sleep, dreamless oblivion. It was evening before I came out of it and I woke completely myself. I had a moment or two before memory caught up with me and I could get myself oriented, but most of that was confusion born of unfamiliarity.

I woke in what I immediately recognized was an office. I saw a desk and desk lamp. I saw filing cabinets. There was a man behind the desk, but since the light from the desk lamp fell on the desk and he was in the shadows behind it, I was seeing him only as the shape of a man. I was lying on a leather sofa with a cushion under my head. I was wrapped in a wonderfully light and soft woolen blanket. I woke enamored of that blanket.

My loafers were off my feet and stood neatly arranged on the floor beside the sofa. The waistband of my slacks seemed loose. Exploring under the blanket, I found that it had been undone. Every measure had been taken for my sleeping in comfort. I stretched and, feeling my slacks slipping down, I hauled them up and fastened the waistband.

The man spoke out of the shadows.

"You had a good sleep," he said.

I knew the voice. It was the last voice I could remember. I was in the police station. It was the inquisitor.

"Best sleep I ever had," I said. "Did you hear my prayers and tuck me in?"

"I did what I could to make you comfortable."

"Thank you."

"When did you eat last?"

"Last night," I said. "Dinner last night. I don't know how long I've been sleeping."

"About six hours. It's evening, after eight."

"Sorry I passed out on you," I said, "but I told you I was in no shape."

"I understand. You had a big night. Hungry?"

I hadn't come around to thinking of it, but there are things about which I am suggestible. It took no more than his saying the word. On the instant I was ravenous.

"Come to think of it," I said, "I am—more like starved."

"I was thinking about supper," he said. "I'll have it brought in for both of us. Meanwhile there's always coffee going in the detectives' room. Would you like a cup?"

"I don't want to be any trouble," I said.

It seemed good tactics to act like a guest until I had definite indication that I was something else.

"We've never had anyone here who was less trouble. You slept like an innocent baby. Sugar? Cream?"

"No sugar, thank you. Black."

He shouted a few words of Dutch. Temporizing, I stayed under my blanket and shut my eyes. It wasn't more than a minute before the coffee came. The aroma hit me, and more on reflex than on anything else I sat up and reached for the cup. Along with it there was a plate of sugar cookies.

"Black coffee on an empty stomach makes ulcers," the inquisitor said. "Eat with it. It won't spoil your appetite."

I did as I was told, but behind the coffee and the cookies my mind was beginning to turn over. It came up with some thoughts about the well-known good-cop-bad-cop routine. I was wondering when the bad cop would be coming to bat.

"Am I under arrest?" I asked.

"Why should you be under arrest?"

"You picked me up at my hotel. You brought me here. You didn't return me to my hotel to sleep in my own bed. You kept me here."

"You were exhausted, Mr. Erridge. You were in a state of collapse. To have put you to the further effort of returning to your hotel, going up to your room, I couldn't do that. It would have been cruel and inhuman."

"You are very kind," I said.

"We are not often appreciated."

"Then I'm free to go?"

"I'd like you to stay to supper with me. We have still to talk, Mr. Erridge."

"I'm a stranger here," I said.

"And very highly regarded. I have been assured by your friends that you will give me all the help you can."

I wanted to ask what friends. He couldn't mean Julie and Steve. That left Van Mieris, and at his dinner table I had come to know Fredrik Dorstman. I dropped the Van Mieris name.

"You are well connected, Mr. Erridge, and he thinks well of you."

"And I of him. He's a fine gentleman."

"In Amsterdam you keep other company as well."

"A young lady. She's beautiful, intelligent, and excellent company. All work and no play . . ."

He chuckled.

"Last night you had so much play that it made you very dull," he said.

"She's a very young lady," I said. "I hate to admit it even to myself, but I'm forced to believe that I'm not as young as I once was."

"Nobody is," he said. "It's true of all of us. It begins even in the first minutes after we are born."

"It's long after that before it begins to bite," I said.

I knew that such chit-chat couldn't be carried on forever, but I was happy to ride along with it as long as it might last. Even as I was having the thought, he broke away from it.

"You will give me the young lady's name and address," he said.

"I see no reason why I should."

"Any reason why you shouldn't?"

"The way I was brought up," I said.

I expected him to press, but he didn't. I had no delusion that he wouldn't be coming back to it. This was going to be the technique. We would have stretches of easy, relaxing talk, but I would be better not relaxed. I had to be prepared to bring my guard up whenever he would pounce. The kids were out there and they were asking for it. Sooner or later he was going to have them.

I could see no way that he wouldn't, but it wasn't going to be through Erridge. However wrongheaded they might have been, and I wasn't certain that they were even that, I was absolutely convinced that they couldn't have been more right in heart.

The supper came in and there was a lot of it. He was himself a hearty eater and he couldn't have been more assiduous in urging me to stoke up. He didn't pounce even once while we were eating, and we were eating too much to have it over quickly.

It was only when we had finished our coffee and he had brought out the inevitable Dutch cigars that he returned to the business at hand. He spoke out of a cloud of cigar smoke and, enveloped in my own cigar-smoke cloud, I listened. Now he was asking no questions. He had shifted to telling me.

"We first became aware of you, Mr. Erridge," he said, "when two of my men came on you down in a canal with an effigy of a prominent and respected Amsterdam citizen. The effigy, since it was light and slow to absorb water, persisted in floating. The officers who pulled it and you out of the canal are unable to say what you were doing down there. You may have been trying to salvage the effigy from the water or you may have been attempting to make it sink out of sight."

I was ready to set him straight on that one point, but he wasn't waiting for me to speak. He went straight on.

"At the time," he said, "the officers, and I cannot fault them for it, assumed that you were trying to salvage the thing from the canal. It is only what you did later that brought the matter into question. You had been injured. Your head was bleeding. You were taken to a hospital where you were given the necessary medical attention. It was to be assumed that from the hospital you would go to your hotel and go to bed. It was to be expected that you'd had what any man would feel had been a full night."

At that point he paused. There was nothing in the manner of his pausing to indicate that he was waiting for me to say something, but the opportunity was there and I took it.

"You're speaking," I said, "of what might have been expected of any sensible man. You must remember that I had been knocked insensible. So there were aftereffects. I was restless, hopped-up."

"Yes, Mr. Erridge," he said. "I recognize that you are a man of remarkable vitality. It's been apparent to me that you went on much past your strength, pushing yourself until you collapsed. You must remember that I was witness to your collapse."

I had something to say to that, but I took the precaution of softening it with an introductory chuckle.

"When I reached the end of my strength," I said, "you took over. I think it's fair to say that you pushed me to the point of collapse."

"Fair enough," he said, "but it was only after you had already pushed yourself too far. That brings us to what you did after you left the hospital. You were next brought to our notice when we had a report of a hanging. A citizen called it in, and the men who went out on it thought they were going to a suicide. On what the citizen had reported, it was taken to have been a suicide of the most extraordinary theatricality. The thought of a man hanging five effigies in preparation for hanging himself among them should, I suppose, have given us pause. We should perhaps have recognized at once that it was excessive."

He paused again and this time it seemed like an expectant pause. I had a feeling that he was inviting me to speak. I thought it better that I shouldn't. So I left it at elaborating my cigar-smoke screen with a few neat smoke rings. He blew some of his own and, as his and mine met in midair, he spoke again.

"When my men arrived on the scene and brought down the body and the five effigies that had been hanging on one side of it and the other, they quickly recognized that what they had was not a suicide but a murder. You saw the body. Now that you are completely yourself, you will see it again. On this second viewing, you may recognize it."

I did speak to that. "I think not," I said. "I grant you that I was having a hard time keeping my eyes open, but I did see it. It was nobody I know. After all, I know very few people here in Amsterdam."

"You will see it again," he repeated. "You may or may not have noticed and you may or may not have understood, but the marks on the dead man's neck are clear testimony to the way he died."

He described the band of bruise and the sharper mark that ran through the center of it.

"The broad bruise mark," he said, "was made by the rope on which he had been hanging. The other mark was made by the wire used for garroting him. The garroting killed him. The hanging only put his corpse on display. It is possible for a man to hang himself. For a man to garrote himself, that's an impossibility. You follow my reasoning?"

"I follow," I said.

"Good. The citizen who alerted us to this extraordinary occurrence lives just across the street. He is an early riser and every morning on rising he stands at his open window and does exercises. This morning he did no exercises because when he went to his window he was confronted with the spectacle of six hanged men dangling across the street. He left his window but only long enough to fetch his binoculars. With the glasses he saw that they were not six hanged men but only one man and five effigies. Recognizing that even one hanged man is more than enough, he telephoned us and reported the matter. Returning from the telephone, he remained at the window with his glasses waiting for our arrival at the scene."

Again he paused, and now I had a shrewd idea of what would be coming next. I decided that I could wait for it. It was obvious that I couldn't forestall it. This time he was before me in blowing the smoke rings. I contributed a few of my own. I hoped they might be representative of the controlled calm of the innocent.

"Shortly before my men reached the scene," he said, "a car drove up and stopped in the street below him. There was a man and a woman in the car. The man had a bandaged head. The man at the window could well understand that anyone just happening to drive through would notice the six hangings and would be stopped by the sight of them. It was his impression, though, that this man and woman hadn't happened by through accident. It seemed to him that they had come with the specific objective of seeing what there was to see, that they had come with some foreknowledge that there would be something to see. This impression was confirmed for him when he heard the sirens of the approaching police cars. The man and woman down below had also been using glasses for observing the hangings. At the first sound of the police sirens they left, driving away at most excessive speed. The man at the window had recognized at first sight that the car was a Porsche. Porsches are eye-catching and one doesn't see so many of them that, when one comes along, it goes unnoticed. The same may be said of men with bandaged heads. When it appeared to him that the Porsche was speeding off to elude the police, he followed it with his glasses and was able to make a note of its license plate."

When he paused this time it was to wait me out. He waited and, when I said nothing, he did ask a question.

"You have nothing to say, Mr. Erridge?" he asked.

"Must I tell you I was there?" I said. "You already know I was there."

"And not waiting for the police."

"I had the young woman with me," I said. "She had already experienced more shock than I would have wanted for her. It was important to me that I spare her any more."

"Which is why you will have to tell us her name and address."

"I can't see where that follows."

"It follows, Mr. Erridge. I can assure you that it follows."

"I'm sorry," I said. "She has nothing to do with this. You will have to manage without her."

Leaving it at that, he returned to his narrative. I had no delusion that he would be leaving it for good. He was a patient and persistent man. I was going to be a stubborn one.

"Everything was brought to me," he said, "the man's statement, the body, the five effigies, the six ropes, the sixth effigy—recognizably a duplicate of the other five even though water-damaged, the report of the removal of it and you from the canal, and the report of your story of having been knocked on the head and robbed. It immediately occurred to me that Mr. Erridge with his head bandaged and the man with the bandaged head who sped away in the Porsche were one and the same. I was not left to speculate for long, since the license number of your car is recorded on the registration card they have for you at your hotel. I have since learned from your distinguished friend that you are acquainted with the original of those six effigies. You met him at dinner in the home of your distinguished friend. In the light of all that, you can understand why it is necessary that we talk."

What he was saying, of course, was that it was necessary that *I* talk. He had spoken his piece. There wasn't much that I could add to it. There was, in fact, just about nothing except what I was determined I was not going to tell him.

I had myself braced for his questions, but he was holding back on them. First it was a return trip to the morgue and my second viewing of the dead man. That brought him nothing because it brought me nothing. The man had been nobody I knew. He wasn't even anyone I could remember just having seen around.

We returned to the office, where he settled the two of us in with fresh cigars. My assertion that I had no recognition of the dead man he had accepted without comment. It was only when he was once more enveloped in his smoke screen that he spoke again.

"I was not depending on you for an identification of the murdered man," he said. "When you saw him before, he had not yet been identified, but that was done while you were sleeping. His name is Groen, Dirk Groen. You might say that the hanging was a homecoming for him."

I took that to mean that the police knew the man as a participant in the demonstration they had broken up the day before.

"A homecoming?" I asked. I was giving nothing away.

He explained about the buildings—the planned demolition, the planned construction of a parking garage.

"As you must be aware," he said, "the six effigies are caricatures of Fredrik Dorstman. He is the owner of the buildings and he is going to build the garage. The buildings were long standing vacant and they had been occupied by squatters. In preparation for the demolition the squatters were evicted. It was necessary to use force to get them out. Dirk Groen was one of the squatters."

"It couldn't have been necessary to kill him to get him out," I said.

"The police handled the eviction, Mr. Erridge. Some of the people resisted and had to be carried out bodily. Nobody was killed and nobody was injured. Dirk Groen, furthermore, was not among those who resisted."

"Until he tried to get back in?" I asked.

"He may have tried to go back in. Whether he did or not is unlikely to have anything to do with his death, not if you consider the circumstances of his death. There is a curious fact about Dirk Groen. He was at one time in the employ of Fredrik Dorstman. His employment was terminated when Mr. Dorstman charged him with embezzlement. Groen stood trial but the evidence was insufficient. From that time on, however, he was not regularly employed, just manual labor, a day here and a day there."

"Poor guy," I said. "Every which way a victim type."

"What makes you say that, Mr. Erridge?"

"Charges that can't be proved lose him his livelihood and now he ends up murdered. Doesn't that make him a man more sinned against than sinning?"

"Just that? You know nothing about him? His name means nothing to you?"

"Only what you have told me," I said. "I met Dorstman one time at dinner. I know nothing about him and even less about his affairs. All I know is what might have come up in dinner conversation, and nothing was said about the buildings he wanted to demolish or about his plans for the site. Certainly nothing was said about any difficulties he might once have had with an employee."

"You are an engineer. You are in Amsterdam on business."

"On a project that may develop into business for me. It's only in the earliest discussion stages."

"The construction of the parking garage?"

"No, and nothing that involves Mr. Dorstman unless it should develop that he will be a silent investor in the project under discussion. That, of course, is a possibility. I was invited to dinner. The other dinner guests may have been men financially interested in the proposed job. They may have been there to look me over. It's been known to happen. Nothing was said of that in the introductions, but that also has been known to happen."

"Very well," he said. "We return to last night. After you were released from the hospital, you rejoined the young lady. I am assuming that it was the same young lady you dined with, or am I wrong?"

"It was the same young lady," I said.

I couldn't see where that would be giving anything away, and playing the gentleman in refusing to divulge the name of one young woman was going to be difficult enough. There would be nothing to be gained from being gallantly reticent about two.

"You rejoined her. Was that by prearrangement?"

"No. It came up unexpectedly."

The fewer lies a man tells, the fewer lies he will have to keep in mind. Mendacity is most successful when it is kept as simple as possible.

"How did it come up?" he asked.

"I telephoned her."

I couldn't be certain that the hotel mightn't have a record of my having made that wee-hour call. He had secured Baby's license number from the hotel desk. Scenting a small trap, I went with the truth.

"Certainly a strange hour for making a telephone call," he said.

"I had just been through a strange experience," I said.

"And telling the young lady about it couldn't wait till morning?"

"I knew that she would want to hear about it and without waiting."

He broke out in a smile. "Am I wrong in thinking we are beginning to do better, Mr. Erridge?" he said.

I had to counter that and quickly. "All along," I said, "we have been doing as well as I've been able to do."

He stayed with the smile. "I cannot agree," he said. "We're beginning to do better."

"That," I said, "may be only because you asked a better question."

"Then I must try for another better question, Mr. Erridge. Now I must ask you why she would have wanted to hear about it and so urgently that it couldn't have waited till morning."

"What brings the young lady and me together," I said, "is a shared interest in the arts."

"Please, Mr. Erridge."

"She is a student of the arts," I said, "and I am a devoted amateur."

"I must insist that you return to the matter at hand," he said.

"It *is* the matter at hand. I am here on business. Business in these stages of preliminary negotiation involves an hour or two of discussion and then perhaps days of waiting before the next meeting. So I am in Amsterdam with much time on my hands. For an amateur of the arts Amsterdam is a great city. There is the Rijksmuseum for Rembrandt, Vermeer, de Hooch, Jan Steen. There is the Van Gogh museum. There is the Rembrandt House. That is how the young woman and I met. That is the reason why we have been seeing each other."

"And this you are telling me is the matter in hand?" he said. His smile had been fading. Now it was all gone.

"If you will let me finish," I said.

"If you are going to talk about museums," he said, "we will never finish."

"People who frequent museums are interested in other art exhibits as well."

"Mr. Erridge," he said. "I must insist. "

"There was to be an exhibit we wanted to see," I said. "It was not going to be on for long. If we weren't early up and out to catch it first thing in the morning, we would almost certainly miss it. So we had an engagement to see it early."

"*That* early?"

"No, not before daylight. It's no good looking at art exhibits in the dark."

"I live here in Amsterdam," he said, "a great city of art. I am no great amateur of the arts such as you seem to be, Mr. Erridge, but I am not totally ignorant. Art exhibits, if they are not in museums, are to be found in art galleries."

"Not always," I said. "Artists today are extending themselves out of the museums and out of the art galleries. There is a man who wraps barrier reefs, hangs a curtain across a mountain gorge, or builds a fence that runs miles and miles across California, fencing nothing. In New York an artist dug a hole in Central Park and filled it up again, creating for the city the memory of a hole. Art of this kind cannot be done in museums or galleries."

"If you will forgive me," he said, "that is the United States. To us Europeans American behavior is not always comprehensible."

"I'm afraid you haven't been keeping up," I said. "Happenings, environmental art—these things are a worldwide movement."

CHAPTER 7

Unprepared to dispute that point with the great amateur, he moved back to what for him was more comfortable ground.

"You had an early-morning appointment with the young lady," he said, "but you'd had an extraordinary experience and you couldn't let her wait till your early-morning meeting to tell her about it. That was the position? I have not misunderstood you?"

"That was the position."

"You will have to explain this urgency," he said.

"We were to go to an outdoor exhibition of sculpture," I explained. I had to bend the truth that much, and even then I was afraid I was treading dangerous ground. "It was to be a show of painted portrait heads done in plaster, heads of a prominent Amsterdam citizen. I had come on such a painted plaster head floating in the canal. Even though it was considerably water-damaged, I recognized it as the head of a prominent Amsterdam citizen I had met the night before at dinner."

"Fredrik Dorstman."

"Recognizable," I said, "even past the water damage."

"I didn't find it recognizable," he said, "not until I was able to compare it with the undamaged copies. Could it be that you had seen this plaster head before?"

That was a question I didn't want to answer, but it was a question I had foreseen. I was prepared for it.

"I don't want to sound boastful," I said, "but I have been keeping up with the current developments in the arts, and it is evident that you have not. It would be astonishing if my eye weren't better attuned to these things than yours."

"All right," he said. "I'm no expert. You are."

It seemed a good spot for a little becoming modesty.

"Only an interested amateur," I said.

"That much ahead of me," he said. "I cannot be interested in the memory of a hole."

"I can sympathize," I said. "I found that one a bit extreme."

I was playing it along as best I could, but I was astonished at the man's patience. I would have expected him to have long since brought out the thumbscrews or some modern equivalent thereof.

"You must still explain the reason for your phone call," he said.

"The young lady had been very keen on seeing the exhibit," I said. "She sees all these things. She hates to miss even one of them. I had to tell her that we might already have been too late. I was afraid that the exhibit had been dismantled. After all, I was reasonably certain that I had seen one of the exhibits and it had already been trashed. I suggested that we move our early engagement to an even earlier time. Day would be breaking by the time we could get to the exhibition place. Even at first light it was possible that it was going to be too late to see anything of what might have remained. If we were to have any chance of catching even part of it, time appeared to be of the essence. She agreed, and we made the earlier start."

"How did you know that there was going to be this exhibition?" he asked.

His tone put clearly audible question marks around the word "exhibition." He didn't have to resort to any of that quote-unquote business or twiddle his fingers in the air.

"The grapevine," I said. "You hang around the museums and the galleries and you hear these things. It's word of mouth in the art district. One person hears it from another and it's passed along. You never remember who you heard it from and he won't remember who he heard it from."

"You don't remember who you heard it from, Mr. Erridge?"

I could hardly tell him that it had come to me not so much through the grapevine as perhaps through the gripevine. I did some quick thinking.

"I can't say I heard it from anyone," I said. "It was more like I overheard it. You know the Rijksmuseum?"

"Even though I don't keep up on the memory of holes."

"You must certainly know Rembrandt's 'Night Watch.'"

"In Amsterdam, Mr. Erridge, even a policeman who knows nothing of art knows the 'Night Watch.'"

He was referring, of course, to that occasion not many years before when a nut attacked the famous canvas with a knife and sliced great slashes in it.

"I suppose," I said, "that room where the 'Night Watch' hangs has always been the most crowded place in the museum. Now, restored and put back on display, it must be that the picture is drawing greater crowds than ever. That room may well be the most congested place in all of Amsterdam."

"So?"

"So, jammed in there with that huge crowd around me

and everybody looking at the 'Night Watch,' I overheard somebody tell somebody else about this outdoor sculpture exhibit there was going to be this morning. He was telling his friend where it was to be and giving him exact instructions on how to get there. I couldn't even see which people in that jam were talking about it, but I overheard the whole thing."

"Americans talking?" he asked. "They were speaking in English?"

"As a matter of fact, no," I said. "Not in English. It was either French or German. I can't remember which, but one or the other. I understand both."

It seemed a good idea to keep this part of it as muddled as possible.

"And you told your young lady?"

"I mentioned it to her," I said. "I thought she would be interested. She had also heard about it in much the same way, and she'd been planning to go. Since I was also interested, we made the date for me to take her in my car."

"We have no laws against attendance at art exhibits, Mr. Erridge. You must explain to me your quick departure from the exhibition. You had come a long way to see it. You had gone without sleep to the point of exhaustion. You had suffered an injury and had given yourself no time to rest and recover from it. Then you were contented with only the quickest of quick looks. Will you tell me that such is the extent of interest for a devoted amateur of the arts?"

"Now that, sir," I said, "is a question that hardly needs answering."

"I would like to hear your answer."

"Like the man who reported the thing to the police," I

said, "I had to use binoculars to see the heads properly. Through the binoculars I saw at once that there was only five sixths of the art exhibit then on view. The remaining sixth I had seen water-damaged. In its place I saw something that was no work of art."

That brought another smile, but this one was soured with sarcasm.

"I would think that for the amateur of the arts as they are practiced today the memory of a man would be more compelling than the memory of a hole."

I rode along with it. "It didn't occur to me to think of it that way," I said. "Perhaps it's because I am just an amateur."

"How did you think of it?"

"I heard the police sirens and it was obvious to me that the police would find it at least strange that, having found me in the canal with one of the effigies, they should find me again when I would be inspecting the other five and the body of a man dead by hanging. Of course, I would have had no trouble explaining, as, in fact, I've had no trouble explaining to you, but I had the young lady with me. I had fallen into this nasty business. I couldn't with good conscience bring her into it. If I may say so, I can't feel that I was wrong about that. It would have been most unpleasant for her, going to the morgue, viewing the body, all of that."

"We are going to have to require it of her, all of that," he said.

"I dare say you will. I see no possible reason for it, but if you find her, I dare say you will. You must expect no assistance from me with that part of it. I will not help you find her. It would be cruel to put her through it, and I refuse to take any part in unnecessary cruelty."

"You must permit me to be the judge of what is necessary and what is not."

"You will make your judgment," I said. "I have made mine."

He was, of course, not happy to leave it at that. He worked on me. He reasoned with me. He mingled cajolery with suggestions of threat. A foreign visitor suspected of impeding a murder investigation could hardly expect that he would be permitted to go on enjoying the hospitality of the country. The business I had in Amsterdam was not likely to prosper if I were to be put out of the country.

I picked up on that. "Am I to be kicked out of the country?" I asked.

I was careful to keep even the least trace of anxiety out of my question. I was challenging him with it.

"Not immediately," he said, throwing the challenge back at me. "You will have time to think about it. I expect that you will come to understand that in a matter of murder you have an obligation to be fully cooperative."

"I understand that," I said. "We differ only in the way we define 'fully.'"

There was more of it, but it left our positions unchanged. When he finally told me that he would keep me no longer but would be talking to me again after I'd had time to think about it, I offered to pay for my supper.

"You were a guest," he said.

"But since I proved an unsatisfactory and unobliging guest," I said.

"I hoped you would be more obliging and I am still hoping for that, but it makes no difference. I had to think of my reputation. To keep you here so that we might talk and to let you starve the while—I could have been accused of police brutality, Mr. Erridge."

I told him that he had been most considerate and that I was sorry that I couldn't be more obliging, but I added that when he had time to think about it, he would recognize that I had done all I could.

"You will solve your murder without inconveniencing the young lady," I said. "I have complete confidence in you."

With something that approached an exchange of compliments we parted. I took a cab to my hotel. In the traffic I had no way of knowing whether or not the cab was being followed, but a car pulled up while I was paying the cabbie and I noticed that the doorman was holding still for the car being left where no doorman would ordinarily permit it. The man who had driven up in that car came into the lobby behind me. I had the thought that I would head into the gents just to determine whether that would have an effect on the man's bladder, but long before I reached it I was waylaid.

Fredrik Dorstman came heaving up out of one of the lobby chairs. At sight of him I had only one thought, and that was freshened admiration for Steve Dale's skill and talent. Good art will do that to a man. You fall into seeing with the artist's vision. I was seeing Dorstman now with Steve Dale's eye. The man was never again going to have any other look for me.

It was no accidental meeting, and he made no pretense that it might be. He had come to the hotel to see me. He had been waiting for me.

"You will come with me into the bar," he said. "We will have a drink."

My first impulse was to shake him off. My head was full

of all the lies I needed to sort out and remember. I was trying to figure a way I could get together with Julie. I wasn't so confident that my patient policeman wouldn't be finding her even without my help. I couldn't hope that he wouldn't find Dale, and with Julie insisting on staying with Dale, I was seeing it as being all too easy. It was going to happen, but I was determined that it would not be through me.

Since it was going to happen, however, I was going to have to find a way of getting to her everything she needed to know. When the time would come for her to be lying to the police, she would need to know just what lies they had already had from me.

I was afflicted with a constantly growing certainty that I had a police tail on me. I couldn't go to her. I couldn't telephone her either. There had been more than enough time for setting up the monitoring of any calls I would make. There had to be a way, and I was going to have to find it and without too much delay. The last thing I needed was for bastard Dorstman to come along and divert me from my problems.

I was on the point of begging off by pleading my bandaged head, but before I'd said anything I was having second thoughts. I had no idea of what the man could have been wanting with me, but I had begun to have ideas of things I could have been wanting from him.

We went into the bar. Dorstman led me to a corner table. It had a RESERVED card on it. The bar was doing great business, but the table Dorstman had taken was well insulated from it by a double row of empty tables, all with the RESERVED cards on them. When an important citizen throws his weight around, he gets results. The setup was obviously prearranged. We were going to talk, and we were going to have well-organized privacy for it.

The man I had been planning to test performed as I'd expected. Our move into the bar had made him thirsty. For us service was immediate. I had to be impressed. I waited only until the waiter had taken the drinks order and I opened up.

"Are you sure you want to be seen with me?" I said. "I'm being watched by the police."

"*You* watched?"

It was astonishment. I was reading it for counterfeit astonishment.

"There's been a murder," I said.

"Dirk Groen?" he said. "Nobody will worry too much about Dirk Groen. The police will go through the motions. They have to, but it's not to be taken seriously. Dirk Groen is no loss."

"With me the police have been taking it seriously," I said.

"Going through the motions, putting on an act. They are good police, so they put on a good act. It means nothing."

"I take it you knew him," I said.

"I knew him. I knew him well, too well. A thief, an incompetent, a ne'er-do-well. He robbed me. We have courts, Mr. Erridge. They have pity only for the criminal and no pity for the victim. He went free. So now he got it. Who should care?"

Seeing this fat-bellied slug as a victim wasn't easy. I tried it for size and I couldn't make it fit.

"Death," I said, "is heavy punishment."

"A man is a bum. He lives with bums, with criminals, with dissidents, with rioters, with thieves. So thieves fall out. If they would kill each other off, all of them, the world would be better for it."

Although there was much that could be said to that, saying any of it to this Fredrik Dorstman would have been to waste the words. A man who holds such bloodthirsty sentiments is not a reasonable person. Trying to reason with him is futile. I couldn't believe that he had sought me out with nothing more in mind than giving me his opinion of the dead man. There had to be something more. I was waiting for it.

The drinks were served and Dorstman waited until the waiter's departure reestablished our reserved-table isolation. Then he asked the question I could guess he had come to ask.

"What do you have against me, Mr. Erridge?" he said.

"Mr. Dorstman," I said, "I would have to know you better before I could have anything against you."

If putting it that way suggested that on knowing him better I might have reason for disliking him, I felt no need to soften it.

"You have been listening to slanders," he said.

"Only what I have been told by the police," I said. "If they are slandering you, you might want to take it up with them."

"What did they tell you?"

The guy was so filled up with paranoia and self-pity that he seemed ready to believe that anything said about him by anyone, even the police, would be slanderous.

"They told me that you own a real-estate parcel here in Amsterdam, old buildings that had been occupied by homeless squatters. They told me that you have had them evict the squatters and that it is your intention to demolish the buildings and replace them with a parking garage.

They also told me that Dirk Groen was one of the evicted squatters. Is any of that slander?"

"A man has a right to do what he likes with his property," Dorstman said. "He has a right to a return on his investment."

I made no comment on that.

"That's all I know about you," I said.

"Of course, it's all you know. So why do you attack me?"

"Perhaps I'm the one who's been slandered," I said. "I'd say it was your turn to tell me what you have been hearing about me."

"I am being held up to public ridicule," he said. "The attack on me is shocking. It's vile. You know what I'm talking about."

"I know that you have been hanged in effigy six times over," I said. "You are referring to that, aren't you?"

"That and the poster, a filthy, obscene poster."

"Yes," I said. "That too. I have seen it."

"You admit it?"

"I have been questioned by the police in the matter of the Groen murder," I said. "In the course of the questioning they showed me the effigies and the poster."

"That's only part of the truth, Mr. Erridge."

He launched into a diatribe. I did nothing to interrupt it. Although what he was saying was way out in left field, it had a basis that was well within the ball park. He knew that there was a young sculptor and a young woman associated with him. He knew that the effigies and the poster were the young sculptor's work. He knew that the sculptor and the young woman were Americans. He either didn't know their names or he was holding that bit of it back.

He knew that I had been down in the canal with one of the effigies and that I had gone with the girl to the demolition site. He even knew that, returning from there with the girl, I had attended what he called "a council of war with those ruffians, those rascals, those Reds, those bums."

There was more, but for the rest of it he was only in the area of things he thought he knew. He didn't, however, present the remaining items as conjectural. He treated them as though they were as factual as the rest of it. There was my bandaged head. He told me that there was only one place where I could have run into that, in the demonstration broken up by the police the previous day at the demolition site. Why had I gone there to demonstrate against him? Why would I get myself mixed up with that gang of hoodlums? Why was I financing them in their lawlessness? Why was I financing them in spreading filth about him?

I tried to set him straight on where I had been when I was knocked on the head, but he was just not going to be convinced.

"I don't know where you picked up all this garbage," I said, "because it is garbage. There's the one item you don't have to take my word for. You can check that with the police. They know where I was and when it was that I was clubbed down. They'll tell you."

He disregarded that. "I'm asking you to stop," he said. "I'm asking you nicely. I'm asking you to stop all this agitation against me. You can do it. All it will take is for you to stop the money."

"That's ridiculous," I said. "The quarrel these people have with you didn't start yesterday. It was going on before I ever came to Amsterdam. You don't have to believe me, but you do have to recognize the facts. I didn't start it because I wasn't here to start it and I have no way of stopping it."

"I'm not a child, Mr. Erridge," he said. "I'm a businessman. I know that bank drafts can be sent through the mails. I know that for money to be given it doesn't have to be coins passed from hand to hand."

"You're working on misinformation," I said. "I'd like to know where you got it."

That won me a sneer. "I'm sure you would like to know," he said. "I have my sources."

"You need better sources. If you've been paying for information, you've been cheated."

"Then you are not going to stop this filth?" he asked.

"All right, mister," I said. "When we started this, you asked me what I had against you. At that point I wasn't crazy about what I had been hearing about you; but, except for thinking you weren't a very nice man, I had nothing against you. I hardly knew you. Now that I know you better, I have a worse opinion of you, but that is neither here nor there. You can't expect everyone to love you. It's even possible that you can't expect *anyone* to love you, but I wouldn't know about that. In any event, what I think of you doesn't matter. There's this campaign against you and you want it stopped. I can do nothing for you. You've come to the wrong man."

"I can have you stopped. I am not without friends. I am not without influence."

"You are without good sense," I said. "How can you have me stopped from something I'm not doing and that I never have been doing?"

"Your business here in Amsterdam," he said. "A word to the right man about this other business you have found for yourself here and you will have no business in Amsterdam."

I pushed my chair back and got to my feet.

"The hell with you, mister," I said. I brought some money out of my pocket and dumped it on the table. "That," I said, "will pay for my drink."

His response was something explosive, but I heard it only faintly behind my back as I walked away from him. Anyhow, it was in Dutch. I wasn't missing anything.

As I was leaving the bar, I took a passing look at the man who had followed us in there. He had been having a beer and he had been making it last. I saw him switch to gulping it. I didn't bother to look back over my shoulder. I knew he would be following me out of the bar.

Now, more than ever, I had to talk to Julie. Fredrik Dorstman knew far too much. Only a small part of what he had poured out at me, he could have had from the police. There was all the rest of it. As he'd said, he had his sources.

There was a line of phone booths in the lobby. It took only the sight of them to have me telling myself I was a knothead. I couldn't phone her from my room, but only because it would be a call that would go through the hotel switchboard. I don't know how it could have slipped my mind that there were pay phones. The police couldn't have every line in Amsterdam tapped.

Even as I was heading for a booth, it occurred to me that they could have her line tapped. I just had the thought and I shed it as quickly as it had come to me. My problem was how I could get to her without leading the police to her. If they had her phone tapped, then it would follow that they weren't needing any leading from me. It would mean that they knew who she was and where they could find her. I could call her from a booth and, just in case her line was tapped, I would only have to be careful of what I would say.

Heading into one of the lobby booths, I was shaping up in my head just what it would be, but I was no sooner in there than I saw it would be no good. The phones in the booths were not dial phones. They were hooked into the hotel switchboard.

I pulled right out and my man came popping out of the adjacent booth. He had also changed his mind about making a call. Coming out of the hotel into Stadhouders-kade, I took note of his car. It was still standing where he had left it, and it was evidently not bothering the door-man at all.

I took the bridge across Singelgracht and on across the small canal beyond to come into Leidseplein. It's a big square and a nonstop madhouse of traffic. It has trolley lines running through it every which way and cars pour-ing in and out in steady streams, not to speak of the throngs of pedestrians that are always dodging through the traffic.

There could hardly have been a better place for shak-ing off a tail, but I wasn't bothering. Around the rim of Leidseplein there is an assortment of beer joints. They had phone booths and in those there would be dial phones and no switchboard the police could have been monitoring. I hit the nearest of the cafes. It had a phone booth and only one. I took it. My tail could report that I'd found a booth and made a call. Small good that would do him. I dialed Julie's number, and while I was waiting for her to come on I was framing what I would say to her. I was half expecting that it would be Dale who would be answering and I was hoping it wouldn't be.

It wasn't. I got Julie.

"Matt calling," I said, and without waiting for anything from her, I went bulling ahead. "I've been thinking," I said. "It's all very well your concentrating on Van Gogh, but you shouldn't be neglecting the old masters. You want to be well rounded."

I can think of girls who would have heard that much and have thought old Matt had gone irretrievably around the bend. Julie was not one of them. The kid was quick-witted.

"What would you suggest?" she said.

"Rembrandt. You should be going to the Rijksmuseum. It's a long time since you last looked at the 'Night Watch.' I mean bellied up against the railing in front of it for a long look. You don't want to just be seeing it in passing and dismissing it because it's so familiar and so popular. That's one great hunk of painting. You should be giving it time, really studying it. Will you do that? It will broaden your vision. You will learn things you need to know. Promise me?"

"I promise," she said.

"First thing tomorrow," I said. "As soon as the museum opens. I know it will be crammed with tourist parties and all those conducted groups with the lecturers to tell them what they are looking at, but that can't be helped. It's always like that. You can't avoid it, and if you get yourself up front right against the railing, it isn't too bad. Up close that way, you can study the brushwork and, even though it's jammed, that way you have all the people behind you. If you concentrate hard enough, they won't bother you."

"They won't bother me," she said. "How's your head?"

Trying to make certain that she was getting the message, I may have been laboring it too much. It occurred to me that she might have been asking if I was in my right mind.

"Like nothing happened," I said. "I had a good sleep all afternoon. It was all I needed. I'm a new man."

"Are you alone?"

"I'm never alone. But about the Rijks, you will go first thing in the morning?"

"I promised," she said. "I keep my promises."

"You'd better," I said. "I'll be there to check up on you."

"Good. Then you can tell me all you know about the old masters. I'm so ignorant."

"I wouldn't call you ignorant," I said. "There are things I can tell you about Rembrandt that you really ought to know."

"Oh, yes," she said. "It will be a great help. You know how it is when you come up for your orals, there's always some joker on the board of examiners who decides to examine you on periods and painters you haven't prepared to talk about."

"That's exactly what I've been thinking," I said. "You have to be prepared on everything or else some professor will catch you out."

"You're so right," she said. "I have been neglecting Rembrandt, but first thing tomorrow morning I'll make a start at setting that right. And the 'Night Watch' is the key picture in his development. First thing tomorrow morning, as soon as the museum opens. I promise."

CHAPTER 8

I wasn't alone. This time my man walked away from a beer even though he'd hardly dented its foam. Out in the melee of the Leidseplein I was tempted to have a try at losing him, but I put the temptation aside. There would be a time for that. For then it was better that I should be the stupid American who could never dream that he was being tailed.

I strolled. I made no sudden moves. I worked at lulling the man into the belief that he was doing a great job and that I was unaware of him.

Up in my hotel room I settled down at the writing desk. I got down on paper a full account of my session with the police and all details of what I'd had from Dorstman. It was to be a full briefing for Julie on just how much I could determine of what the police knew and on just what lies I had told the inquisitor. I urged her to study the lies so that, in the event they should find her and question her, she could match her lies to mine.

I directed her attention to what they knew so that she would be aware of the areas in which it would be best if she went with the truth. Having completed that part of it to my satisfaction, I did an analysis for her of the Dorstman conversation.

I suggested the possibility that he might know more than he had let on to me. Even if unnecessarily, I pointed to all the items he did know. It was clear that they had a traitor in their group. They had been infiltrated and reports were going back to Dorstman. This was something they had to know.

I told her that the police wanted her and that I was determined that I would not lead them to her. I explained that I had established myself with the police as an amateur of the arts and that we could keep in touch by meeting each morning at the railing in front of the "Night Watch." I even said that I would have preferred it if we could have met in the smaller and quieter back galleries where they had the Vermeers, but the "Night Watch" would give us the cover of crowds. That last, of course, wasn't necessary.

It was vanity that led me to put it in. I wanted her to know that I was a man of taste and not a dumb tourist, hooked on publicity.

I was reading over what I had written, checking to make sure that I had left nothing out, when the phone rang. I could think nothing but that it was Julie calling me, and I cursed myself for not having told her I was phoning from a booth. I was asking myself how she could be so stupid as to call me, but then I had to remind myself that she couldn't know that I had been picked up by the police. I thought of not answering, but I quickly thought better of that. The longer I let the thing ring, the more time there might be for the police to zero in on the number that was calling. Once I'd had that thought, I snatched up the phone.

It wasn't Julie. It was Jan Van Mieris.

"How are you?" he said.

"Never better."

"You had an accident."

"Nothing serious. I'm none the worse for it."

"Tough man."

I laughed. "I was hit where I'm toughest," I said. "In the head."

"I feel I should apologize for my city."

"To me? Where I come from?"

"I just heard from Fredrik Dorstman," Van Mieris said. "You met him the other night at my house."

"I met him again tonight. He came around to the hotel to see me."

"He is very angry with you."

"He's stupid."

"That and angry too. He's having a bad time. People laugh at him. He is not a man who can be happy with being laughed at."

"He complained to you about me. Are you telling me to cease and desist?"

"Fredrik is a fool," Van Mieris said. "He's not as big as he thinks he is. Victim of an international conspiracy? The man's an idiot."

"You know that a man's been murdered?" I asked.

"Pitiful. I knew him."

"The murdered man?"

"Groen. He used to work for Dorstman, and that in itself was pitiable. Fredrik is not a good employer."

"I can imagine," I said.

"He ruined that poor man and there is the greatest doubt that he had cause. The evidence was more than scanty, but Dorstman was implacable. So the poor man lost everything—his livelihood, his wife, and now murdered. Dorstman should have a lot on his conscience."

"The wife?" I asked. "The murder?"

"Indirectly," Van Mieris said. "The wife not so indirectly, but the murder indirectly."

He gave me his thinking about the murder. If Dorstman hadn't thrown Groen out of his job and hadn't hounded the man so persistently, Groen would never have been reduced to homelessness. He wouldn't have been a squatter. He wouldn't have been living among the lowest elements. He would have gone on in his lower-middle-class status among people who do not kill. The man was not equipped to deal with people at the level to which he'd fallen.

The murder, therefore, Van Mieris was saying, was a result of Groen's ruin, even if a remote one. Groen's loss of his wife had been far less a remote thing.

"She left him," Van Mieris said. "Dorstman accused him and had him arrested. The woman just up and left him. She waited for nothing. He was in trouble, so she walked out on him."

"Is a wife like that any great loss?" I asked.

"She was the wife he had. She was a hard woman and a mean one, but she was the wife he had. She's a beautiful woman. Maybe she was the only success poor Groen ever had, a beautiful wife. She's a German. She just packed up and went back to Aachen. Germans seem to be like that, either they are too hard or too soft."

"I've known some medium-boiled Germans," I said.

"Maybe those don't come to Holland."

"Dorstman said that a word from him to you . . . ," I said.

"I've had his word, a whole lot of words. I don't listen to fools. I've been thinking you might do me a favor if Dorstman is right and you know the artist."

"Dorstman thinks I turned the guy on and he wants me to turn him off. Can that be what you have in mind?"

"Dorstman says you know him. Dorstman can be wrong about that. He has a great talent for being wrong. I was just thinking that if he is right about it, you could ask the artist if he would be willing to sell me one of his heads of Dorstman and his cartoon of Dorstman with the automobile. I have seen photographs. People took photos of the poster and they are all over Amsterdam. Pictures of the heads are in the papers. I am a collector. If you know the artist, could you tell him I'm interested?"

I couldn't feel comfortable about lying to Van Mieris. With the police it had been different, as it had also been with Dorstman. Those were adversary relationships, but I liked Jan Van Mieris. Whether the job he was considering came through or not, he and I had been on the way to being friends. I dodged it.

"The poster and the heads are in the hands of the police," I said. "I saw them at the police station. Perhaps you should ask them—what disposition they will be making of them."

"They will be going back to the artist," Van Mieris said. "They are his property."

"The police seem to think that they are evidence in the Groen killing," I said.

"They can't go on thinking that for very long. They are bound to release them to their owner."

"I suppose so," I said, "but surely there would be nothing to be done until they do."

"The poster will have to wait until they release it," Van Mieris said. "But one of the heads. There were six. If the sculptor still has the mold, he could cast one for me."

"You'd have to find him," I said.

"Yes. I'll make inquiries. I am not unknown in the galleries and among the dealers. They should know the man's style. I wouldn't have bothered you about it if Dorstman hadn't been so certain. I should have known better. The man is an idiot."

"It was no bother," I said. "It's been nice talking to you."

"You must come to dinner again," he said. "My wife will call you and we won't have the idiot, Fredrik. We had him the other night only because we had dined with him and my wife insisted that he had to be paid back. Women have such ideas."

I pulled out another sheet of the hotel writing paper and added to what I'd previously written a full report on this telephone call. I suggested that Julie tell Dale that he had a customer.

"It will be his decision," I wrote, "but if he will trust my opinion, which he probably won't, it seems to me that there could be worse ideas than his seeing Jan Van Mieris. Van Mieris is a good man and he packs a lot of influence. In this present jam Dale may find a friend in high places helpful."

I folded the sheets of what I had written and I wasn't happy with what I had. There was too much of it. It bulked too big. I needed something much more compact. I read the whole thing through, looking for stuff I could cut, but that was no good. I had been pretty concise. There was nothing there that they didn't have to know.

I harked back to my professional beginnings and thought of a way I could reduce it. I just had to return to being a draftsman. I had been real good at the minute lettering you have to do on blueprints. I hadn't lost the knack. It was far more time-consuming than the quick scrawl, but it could be done. I pulled out a fresh sheet of paper and painstakingly copied everything I had written. I can't say I was keeping it so small that it could have served for doing the Lord's Prayer on the head of a pin, but I held it down.

I also caught up with the simple idea of writing on both sides of the paper. I was a long time over it, but the result was great. I had every last word of it and compressed into just a single sheet well filled on both sides.

There was a lot of it, far more than would have been done on a full set of blueprints. By the time I had finished, my head was aching and my eyes were on fire. A long-time Simenon fan, I remembered that Maigret always took beer for a headache. I had a beer up on room service. Since it couldn't be expected to do anything for my eyes, I didn't wait up to see what it might do for my headache. I got into bed and went to sleep. So I'm still just taking Simenon's word on the headache cure.

In the morning I gave myself an early start. There was something I was going to have to do before it would be opening time at the Rijksmuseum. Since the hotel lobby wasn't crowded, I should have been able to spot my faithful follower. He wasn't there, and outside the car wasn't standing where it had been all evening. I wanted to think that inconvenience had been called off, but I wasn't ready to assume it. That there had only been a change of shifts was far more likely.

I started off on foot, crossing the canals to the Leidseplein. It was going-to-work time and the big square was at its most frenzied. Several men had gone over the bridges in my wake. They couldn't all have been following me but, even though there wasn't a familiar face in the lot, there was nothing to tell me that one among them wouldn't be my replacement tail.

I drifted around in the Leidseplein for a while and then, picking the line that went to the railroad station, I made a quick jump onto a trolley car. There is a peculiarity to riding an Amsterdam trolley that I have never encountered anywhere else. The cars have two doors. One is up front alongside the man who doubles as driver and conductor. The other is at the middle of the car and it is unguarded.

There is nothing unusual about that arrangement. In other cities, however, the door at the front is for entrance and the middle door for exit. In Amsterdam both are used both ways. In fact, almost nobody enters by the front door. They mostly come flooding on at the middle of the car.

The rules say you go forward and pay your fare, but not everyone fights his way through an aisle crowded with standing passengers. It's far less exhausting—not to speak of being more economical—to jump on at the middle and leave at the middle without ever having gone forward to trouble the driver with your money.

I have been told that on occasion an inspector boards a car and asks to see the little tickets given on payment of the fare. A passenger caught without a ticket is subject to a fine, but for daily riders it could perhaps be a good gamble. Enough free rides could cover the occasional fine and still leave a profit.

I had myself embedded in the crowd when I made my jump. It took me on through the middle door, and I worked my way to the front and paid my fare. There I came face to face with one of the men I had seen in the pack that had been behind me when I was crossing the canals. Three or four trolleys on this same line had come through the Leidseplein during the time I had been fooling around in the square.

I rode to the end of the line. You have to know that railroad stations in other parts of the world are nothing like ours back in the States. In Europe rail travel is big. Stations, for all their great, cavernous size, seethe with people. At that hour of the morning, when commuter trains were disgorging great masses of people on their way to work, the Amsterdam station was aswarm.

I rushed into the station and the man I had spotted rushed in after me, but he wasn't running for a train any more than I was. I went through to where I had a good clear view of the rows of tracks and platforms, and I waited there till I spotted a train round in at the far end of the track. I watched for it to choose its platform and moved over there as though I were about to meet someone who would be coming off the train.

The train oozed in along the platform and came to a stop. Passengers came off it on the run. They came about ten abreast. It was like the start of a marathon. Just as they started through the gate, I made my move. I sprinted across the face of the gate. I took a glancing kick in the ankle from one of the front runners as he brushed past behind me. My man, however, was stranded on the other side of the stream of racing commuters. I didn't even try to see what he might have been doing in his effort to cope.

I had nothing to worry about on that score. There would be no way he could make it across. The rush of humanity that was separating us may not have had the weight of a cattle stampede, but it was more than enough for my purpose. I ran with the commuters and with them

I left the station. Since they were for the most part racing for trolley cars, I was able to grab a cab without fighting for it. I told the driver, "Rijksmuseum," and we were off down Damrak.

We got to the museum a good fifteen minutes before it was to open. I was calling that perfect timing. Even though I was certain that my maneuver at the railroad station had been a brilliant success, I have never been one to underestimate police officers. If my man was to catch up with me, he would have done it during that wait for opening hour. He never showed.

That left me only one thing to dim my glow of self-satisfaction. If there had been a tap on Julie's phone, the police could be waiting for us inside the museum. I had done some previous thinking about that, of course, and I was ready to put it away with the thought that, if they did have a tap on her phone, they would now be having no need of using me for leading them to her. A tap could only mean that they had known who she was and where they could find her.

By the time the doors had opened, however, I had something else to bother me. I had expected that among the eager early-comers waiting for the doors to open I would be seeing Julie. I had been hoping that she had gotten the message and that she would stay away from me until we could come together in that crowded exhibition room where the "Night Watch" was on view.

I didn't see her. She wasn't among the people waiting at the doors. I tried to tell myself that she would still be coming, that she wouldn't be breaking the promise she had made to me; but I had a picture of the kid torn between her inclination to trust me and Steve Dale's powerful disinclination. I could all too well imagine the arguments he might have been throwing at her. I had to tell myself that his arguments could have prevailed.

Since I had an admission card and didn't have to line up to pay the entrance fee, I was able to beat even the conducted-tour parties through the turnstiles. Inside I made straight for the one upstairs gallery. Arriving in the van of the crowd, I had no problem about taking up my position at the brass rail that had been installed against the possibility of another demented slasher.

The mob came pouring in after me and Julie was not with them. When she came, if she was coming, little Julie was going to have the devil's own time working her way up to where she could stand beside me at the rail.

I wanted to turn and watch for her but, even more, I didn't want to make myself conspicuous. Standing in the front row of that mob, where nobody had eyes for anything but the painting, I couldn't turn my back on it to peer over the heads of the crowd. I couldn't even do more than a most occasional quick head turning for glances back over my shoulder.

I was, therefore, unaware of him until he had pushed in beside me, opened his sketchbook against the rail, and begun blocking in a quick sketch copy of the captain of the Watch Company. He never looked my way. His gaze darted back and forth between the canvas and the sketch copy he was doing.

I had no problem about looking his way. Anytime an artist takes to sketching in public he will have curious strangers looking over his shoulder. Erridge was the most curious of curious strangers. Looking over his shoulder, I had my lips no more than an inch away from his ear.

"I expected Julie," I whispered.

He darted his hand into the pocket of his jacket and

brought out an eraser. On his way out of his pocket, however, he made a quick dive into mine. I felt his hand plunge in there and come out again. He used the eraser to erase a bit that didn't need erasing. I had seen enough of Steve Dale's work to know that the guy was good. Watching him sketch, I was ready to call him more than good.

I had my sheet of paper with its minute writing rolled up in my hand. I pushed the paper into his jacket pocket. He chose that moment to return the eraser to his pocket. I suppose an artist does need hands that move quickly and precisely. Certainly Dale's hand did. His met mine in his pocket and he gave mine a quick squeeze.

Speaking well above a whisper this time, I admired the sketch he was doing.

"Gee," I said. "You're good, man. You're real good. I bet there aren't many people who can do that."

"Thanks," he said. "I'm doing it for my girl. She wanted to come with me, but I wouldn't let her. If she sees me doing it, it won't be a surprise."

An American woman tourist was standing the other side of Dale. I can't always spot them on sight, but if they wear hairnets I can't miss.

"That's wonderful," she said. "I wish I was your girl."

"Line forms on the right, lady," Dale said.

"I'm on your right," the woman said.

"And first on line."

Have you ever noticed? Sketching in public is like walking a cute dog. It's great for pickups. Dale took to grinning all over his face. He was playing along with it as though his heart was in it. She twinkled and he twinkled. Flirtation with a dame was a lot better than just talking to some guy. I don't know what he would have done for a way of giving me my quick dismissal if that dame hadn't popped up, but she was there and he was making use of it.

I pulled away from the rail, worked my way out through the crowd, and hunted up the men's room. In the privacy of a booth I fished the folded paper out of my pocket. It was a note from Julie.

"Dear Matt," she had written. "I did want to come and I know I promised, but Steve's gone all macho and said I couldn't. I wasn't going to pay any attention to him but, when he insisted that if I went he would be coming too, I knew there was no way I could stop him doing that. He insists that if either of us is to be there, it must be him. So it would have been Steve or the both of us. Both of us would be no good. If the police should be there and arresting people, one of us would be better on the loose to try to do something about it. So that's why Steve has come and I haven't. We now know who the dead man was and it makes it worse, if this horrible thing could be worse. We knew him. He was a sweet man, horribly down on his luck. When I heard, I thought he must have committed suicide. He had plenty of reason for it, but Steve says it would have been physically impossible and I suppose he must know. Since he hung the effigies, he does know what getting the dummies up there involved. Life is too cruel. We are heartbroken for the poor man, and it's unbearable that someone should have sneaked in after Steve had hung the effigies and had come away from there and perverted Steve's work so disgustingly. I'm sorry. I'm sorry about everything."

She signed it "Julie."

I left the museum feeling more than a little sour and more than a little angry. I wasn't ready to believe in Steve Dale as the shining knight, totally dedicated to protecting

Julie. If anybody was going to walk into a police trap, he was going to be the one; but he couldn't be so stupid that he wouldn't know that it wasn't going to be forever before the police got a line on him. They would be coming after him. Since it seemed inevitable that they would be finding Julie with him, I was asking what his protection might be worth.

As I cooled down a bit, I began to see it from his point of view. My thinking was now colored by what I'd heard from Van Mieris. He was confident that through his gallery and dealer connections he would be able to find Dale. It seemed to me that what Van Mieris could do in those areas the police could also do, and it seemed a certainty that they would already be doing it.

Thinking about it, however, I saw a possibility that Steve Dale might know something Jan Van Mieris couldn't know. It was possible that Dale had been making no effort to sell his work in Amsterdam. It was even possible that he had made no effort to sell his work anywhere. I am interested, but I am not so much a gallery buff that I would have heard of every young artist who was exhibiting somewhere in the world. So the fact that I had never heard of Dale didn't mean anything, but, on the other hand, it could have meant a lot. The kid was well-heeled. It could even be that he was not interested in selling. More than that, it could have been that he kept himself so busy modeling and drawing propaganda material for the causes he espoused that he had been doing nothing else.

I'd had a good dose of his contempt for money, and I knew it was the kind of contempt possible only to a young fellow who had always had too much of it. Taking it that way, I could understand that he would have been thinking that the police wouldn't ever catch up with him and that the only danger would be from a trap set by Matthew Erridge, spy and *agent provocateur*.

Of one thing I felt certain. I had been dealt out of the game. Barring the unlikely possibility that something further might come up that I would feel they had to know, I now had no reason to make any further effort at keeping in touch with them. If Dale was right and it was not going to be easy for the police to catch up with him, then the time had come for me to bow out. Unless I stayed away from them, inevitably at one time or another I would be leading the police to them.

I wandered down to the Van Gogh museum. It's a short wander. The museums are all but side-by-side. I didn't think I'd find her there, but there was just the chance that she would be where I'd first met her, looking at that great landscape. I had not the slightest doubt that I had shaken my tail. I expected that I'd be picking him up again as soon as I returned to the hotel or even if I went around to the garage to pick up the Porsche, but, pending that, I was clear of him.

I had nothing in mind but saying goodby to her and telling her that, when this thing cleared up, I was hoping we could meet again. I headed straight for the landscape. Even though I was in anything but the mood for it, it grabbed me. When a thing is that good, it makes your mood.

It had been the slimmest of slim hopes, but she wasn't there. I toured the whole museum just on the chance, but with no luck. I could imagine that she was at home, waiting for Dale to come and report and fearful that he wouldn't be coming. I wasn't going to go around there. It would have been too much of a risk even though I was confident that for the time I was tailless.

I have never felt more at loose ends. I left the museum and wandered the streets, walked along the small canals where at every window of every house there was a window box overflowing with flowers. It was herring season and the vendors were out with their carts. I lunched like a native, eating herring in the street. I stopped in at a cafe and had a couple of drinks, and then I just went on drifting for a few hours through the early afternoon. Eventually finding myself on Leidsegracht, I was back in the neighborhood of my hotel. It occurred to me that I had been out of there before the mail had come in and that I should be checking for letters. Julie Grant and Steve Dale weren't the whole of my life. There was stuff that should have been coming through from the office back in New York, business things I'd have to act on.

There was mail, but I didn't catch up with it until later. There was also Julie. Although a quick glance around the lobby showed me neither of my plainclothes familiars, there were plenty of guys hanging around and there was no guarantee that there hadn't been another change of shift. I tried to pretend that I hadn't seen her. I headed for the desk, but before I had reached it, she came running after me and she was tugging at my arm. She was white-faced and I could see that she had been crying.

"Matt," she said. "Matt, please."

There was no way I could go on pretending she wasn't there.

"This is crazy," I said. "The police are watching me. Didn't Dale give you my note?"

"They won't be watching you anymore," she said. "They have Steve. They've arrested him."

I could think only one thing. They had picked him up at the Rijksmuseum and she had come to tell me it was my fault. I was trying to think how it could have been, but I couldn't pull away from the thought that somehow it had been.

"I wasn't followed to the museum," I said.

I wasn't trying to tell her I wasn't responsible. I was just thinking aloud, working at understanding it.

"It wasn't at the museum," she said. "He went to the police station."

"Turned himself in?"

"No, but it comes to the same thing. He went there and they've arrested him."

"If he wasn't turning himself in," I asked, "what did he go there for?"

Hold on to your hat. You're not going to believe this. I had one helluva time coming around to believing it myself. He had come home from the museum and they had read my note together. What I had written about Jan Van Mieris had given him ideas. The police were holding his property, the six effigies and the poster. He wasn't just going to leave them there without putting in his legitimate claim for them.

"I told him he was crazy," she said. "I told him that they would arrest him, but he said he wasn't going to hide out for something he hadn't done. He said hiding out was making him look guilty just as sneaking out of the country would have made him look guilty. If he didn't go and make his legitimate claim to his property, the police would be thinking he had a reason for not doing it and there would be only the one reason they could possibly think of. By going in and making his claim, he was going to show them he was innocent."

"Not innocent of creating a public disturbance," I said.

"They've arrested him and they're holding him," she said. "Do you think it can be only for that?"

"It can be that it gives them a good reason for holding him while they are investigating the murder," I said.

"I have nobody else to turn to," she said. "Isn't there something you can do to help him?"

"We'll go up to my room and do some telephoning."

A sneaky way of getting a girl up to your hotel room? Scout's honor, I never thought of it at the time. In retrospect I have been wondering whether Erridge could have been slipping, but enough of that. Up in the room I called Van Mieris. I told him that if he still wanted to get in touch with the artist, I knew where the man was.

"Give me his name and address," Van Mieris said. He couldn't have been more eager. "Has he a telephone? I'll get through to him right away."

I told him where Dale was and how he had come there.

"So they've arrested him," he said. "For the police that's a reflex action. It's a stupidity but, except at the very simplest level, all reflex actions are stupidities."

"I'm going to inform the American Embassy," I said. "Have you any suggestions of anything else I can do for him?"

"Don't call your embassy," Van Mieris said. "You know embassies. They don't like it when one of their nationals involves himself in the local problems of a foreign country. It embarrasses them. Embarrassment will make them unsympathetic. Don't do anything. Just leave this in my hands. I'll have him released. But tell me. How did you find him?"

"It happens that I know his girl," I said. "When he was arrested she came to me in the hope that I might be able to help."

"Tell her she mustn't worry. Is she with you now?"

"She is. We're at my hotel."

"Stay there. Get her a cup of tea. I'll bring him to her."

Coming away from the phone, I filled Julie in on what I'd had from Van Mieris. She wanted to believe and she was afraid to believe.

"Do you think he can do it?"

"He talked as though it was a certainty. He's big stuff. He pulls a lot of weight in this town and he's seeing himself on the way to being the great Steve Dale's patron."

"Dorstman's big stuff and he'll be wanting Steve's hide."

"I've seen them together," I said. "They're not in the same league. If Jan Van Mieris so much as looks Dorstman's way, Dorstman starts fawning."

She thought about it for a moment. When she spoke, it sounded like a change of subject.

"I'm crazy," she said.

"Crazy about Dale?"

"Just crazy. I wanted him out, and now, when he may be, I don't know that I do want it. I'm scared, Matt."

"Scared of what?"

"One of the crowd has been reporting to Dorstman. From what you say Dorstman knows, it can't be anything else. Also, it has to be one of the crowd who murdered that poor man, Groen. There's going to be trouble, bad trouble. Are we getting Steve out of jail just so he can get into that?"

"You're thinking that they'll be on a spy hunt. You're thinking that when they think they have their man they'll be doing something violent."

"I know they will and we know that one of them is a murderer," she said. "It can easily be that violent."

"And you're thinking that if he's out of the slammer Dale will be going along with that?"

"No," she said. "Not Steve. The other way. What if they pick on him? What if they go after him?"

"If there's one unlikely candidate in the bunch," I said, "it has to be Steve Dale."

"You know that and I know it," she said, "but we're not them. I can't get it out of my head that Steve is an American. It frightens me."

"And O'Hare is Irish," I said. "Blanc is French. Krakenbaum is German."

"I know, but they are Europeans. It's different."

"The Common Market doesn't go that far, Julie."

"Steve is also rich," she said.

"I've never seen his bank balance, but Piet Claes doesn't look poor."

"There's a difference," she said, "between not being poor and being filthy rich. Steve is filthy rich."

"And they hold it against him?" I asked.

"It affects their thinking and there's no telling how far it can affect their thinking."

CHAPTER 9

Van Mieris hadn't overestimated himself. It took something less than an hour and he delivered Dale as promised. Julie was joyfully all over him for it despite her fears. Van Mieris enjoyed that. What man wouldn't? He also enjoyed being involved. He was having an adventure. It was a refreshing change from his countinghouse milieu. Dale had been released to him. He was standing guarantor for Steve's good behavior. It seemed to me that he was taking the responsibility lightly.

They couldn't have had much time together, but they were coming on like bosom buddies. That Jan Van Mieris should have taken to Steve was not astonishing. I had been prepared for that. That Steve should have so quickly warmed to Van Mieris took more understanding.

Prosperity, power, establishment influence—on no more than suspecting me of such, I had been tagged as the enemy. Van Mieris, who clearly had it and who had demonstrated its workings, should, I was thinking, have been at least as suspect.

Seeing them together and hearing the talk that passed between them, I came to realize that Van Mieris had come on Dale where Dale was vulnerable. Van Mieris had seen the plaster heads and the poster as works of art. He had seen past the subject and past the propaganda aspect to the solid accomplishment. A man capable of such perception was evidently Steve Dale's kind of man. For that he could be forgiven his wealth and power. He was all right. He was of the elect. I couldn't help thinking of history's great array of the most cruelly dictatorial bastards who were also most generous and perceptive patrons of the arts. Since Dale wasn't thinking of that, I wasn't the one to bring it up.

Van Mieris bought the drinks, but even his most valiant efforts to make it a festive occasion succeeded only moderately. Although both Julie and Steve were showing a great warmth of feeling for the man, they were impatient to be away from him. They worked at not letting it show, but it was obvious to me and Van Mieris sensed it. He took off. Although I was assuming that they would want to be shut of me as well, I had no intention of taking off.

That time, however, I was wrong about their feelings, or at least wrong about what I'd been thinking would have been Steve Dale's feelings. I soon discovered that at long last he had come around to trusting me. It may have been that some of his regard for Van Mieris had begun to rub off on Erridge.

I wasn't prepared to believe that he had recognized the fact that I had more than earned his trust. I hadn't betrayed him to the police. The meeting at the Rijksmuseum had not been the trap he had been expecting. To top it all I had put Van Mieris on to him. For one reason or another, however, he had come around to wanting to count me in.

As soon as Van Mieris had left us, Dale launched into something for which I can find no words but Dorstman's— a council of war. He began talking and he was addressing his talk to me.

"Matt," he said. "Okay if I call you Matt?"

"It's the name I respond to best, Steve."

"I'm in over my head, Matt," he said. "I'm scared and I don't know what to do."

"Any need for you to do anything?" I asked.

"This Dorstman spy thing," he said. "The stuff you got from Dorstman—it has to be he's got somebody in our bunch who's reporting back to him."

"I thought you should know that," I said.

"Of course. I had to know it. The trouble is the other guys have to know it too."

"They're your friends. To let them go on in ignorance would be unfriendly," I said.

"One of them isn't," he said. "Dorstman's guy, he isn't any friend."

"So which?" I asked.

"I don't know," he said.

"I can't imagine it of any of them," Julie contributed.

"You tell the fellows," I said. "They'll watch themselves. Of course, it will break things up when every man is suspecting every other man and nobody knowing who can and who can't be trusted."

"Oh, that," Steve said. "That's the least of it. The whole thing's up the creek anyhow what with the murder and Dorstman having us infiltrated. What's scaring me is that somebody's going to get hurt. He'll be hurt bad. I'm thinking even killed, and if it isn't the right man or even if it is . . ."

"Your buddies are that violent?" I asked.

"One of them is no buddy and he's more than violent. He's a murderer."

"And the others?"

"Violent?" Steve said. "Sean and Whitey."

Julie demurred. "Whitey," she said, "is your typical

French intellectual. He'll rationalize violence till he has you thinking it's the greatest thing since love. But it's all in his head, all discourse and no action."

"Don't bet on it," Steve said. "He has it so thoroughly intellectualized that he can do it in cold blood."

They seemed to be too readily in agreement on Sean O'Hare.

"Why Sean?" I asked. "Just because he's Irish?"

"He's Irish and he's here," Julie said.

That I wanted explained. They made quick work of the explanation. Sean O'Hare was in Amsterdam because he was wanted in Ireland both north and south. He had a track record and the kids had it in complete detail.

"What about the others?" I asked.

"Jan Maes," Steve said.

I had already had the story on the fat boy from Julie. Thinking in terms of someone who could have done the hanging, I had written him off on the grounds of inadequate muscle. Thinking about him in this new connection was another matter. I couldn't visualize him as making a success of beating anyone up, but what that type cannot do with his fists, he is all too likely to do very well with a handgun or a knife. I was offering no argument.

"The German?" I asked.

"Kraky?" Steve said. "His talk is bloody enough, but I'd guess it's all talk."

"So far," Julie told him.

"What does 'so far' mean?"

"I've seen it again and again," she said. "Sean embarrasses him. He feels that he has to do something that will make Sean forgive him for not having been part of the Baader-Meinhof bunch. He's walking around just looking for something he can do that will be awful enough so it will establish his manhood in Sean's eyes."

Steve nodded. "Sean rides him," he said. "He calls him Kraky No-Balls. I've never given Kraky a translation."

"Somebody has," Julie said. "He knows."

"If he knows," Steve said, "then it's been getting to him. The guy's idiotically macho, and German macho may not be as explosive as the Latin kind, but it's cold and it's tough."

"Claes?" I asked.

"Cautious," Steve said. "Piet always plays everything safe."

"I don't know," Julie said. "Just because he is that way, it makes him feel that he doesn't quite belong. I wouldn't be too sure that he wouldn't explode at any time, not only to prove himself to the rest of you but even to prove himself to himself."

"You should be looking at them in two ways," I said. "What they might do is only part of it. It's also what they've done."

"We know the record on Sean and Jan," Steve said.

"I'm talking about what isn't yet on the record," I said. "One of your crowd killed Dirk Groen."

They fought against believing that. Even though earlier Julie had said it herself, it seemed to be a thought she just couldn't stay with. Now the two of them were trying to tell me that nobody in their gang had anything against the murdered man. They'd known Groen. They'd liked him. They'd pitied him.

"And somebody killed him," I said, "and it has to be someone who knew about your game last night if he wasn't actually a participant in it. It was someone who knew I was out with Julie last night. He was waiting and

watching when I saw her home, and after that he followed me till I had obliged him by being in a good place
for him to conk me on the head and dump the effigy
where, when it was found, it would be connected to me.
Who owns a panel truck?"

"The truck," Steve said. "It's mine."

"Do you always leave it unlocked and with the key in
the ignition?"

"It's only a truck. Any of the guys wants to use it, it's
there."

"One of the guys used it," I said.

"Dorstman's spy doing Dorstman's dirty work," Steve
said.

"Dorstman," I said, "ruined the poor guy. To follow
that up by having him murdered? That's too extreme.
There has to be a better motive."

"Wrecking my game," Steve said. "Dorstman certainly
wanted that and he did it. Boy, did he ever do it!"

"Still too extreme," I said. "He could have snuffed you
out before you ever got started. His man tells him what
you're doing. He tips the police. The police grab the lot of
you while you're getting your effigies hung and they have
the effigies down before daylight. Nobody ever sees
them."

"So I do another set or I do something else," Steve said.
"I did the poster."

"And now your hands are tied?"

"Now we all have our hands tied," he said. "Now that
murder has come into it, the whole operation has lost its
claim to decency. It doesn't matter whether we did it or
not. The murder smears us."

I had to agree that he was right in that. The murder
had tied his hands and there could be no question but

that it was a result Dorstman would welcome. The fact that this result was produced by the murder of Dirk Groen, furthermore, would mean nothing to Dorstman but that it had been cheaply won. I could readily believe that Dorstman would be happy with the result. I couldn't believe that he had taken such extreme means to bring it about. Unless he had compelling additional reasons, it was wildly out of proportion.

Meanwhile I was thinking that there was something I could contribute that might dissipate the anxiety if not the gloom.

"So the anti-Dorstman campaign has now been abandoned?" I asked.

"It's become a lost cause," Julie said.

"Nobody's going to go on with it now," Steve explained. "We were working up popular sympathy for the squatters. Murder knocks that off, even though it was one of the squatters murdered. People aren't rational about murder."

"You think they should be?" I asked.

"I didn't say they should be. I just said they aren't."

"So you've lost," I said, "and I'm honestly sorry about that, but there's also a bright side. Since the campaign is now finished, there is nothing more for Dorstman's man to be spying on. There's no need for telling any of the rest of your crowd that there was a spy. The way things now stand, there's no need for them to know it and there's no worry about any of them getting any wild ideas of revenge or punishment, is there?"

I had hoped that the two of them might have welcomed that brilliant bit of reasoning. If anything, however, it threw them into an even deeper gloom. Julie moaned, Steve groaned. There was only one thing I could make of that.

"You've already told them?" I said.

They didn't have to answer. Their twin looks of misery were answer enough. I changed the subject.

"You knew this Dirk Groen?" I said.

"A sweet guy," Steve said.

"Pathetic but really a darling," Julie added.

"All of you feel that way about him?"

"The few of us that knew him," Steve said.

He ran through the list. It came to fat, violent Jan and the other natives, with the one exception of Piet Claes. He and the foreigners—the Irishman, the Frenchman, and the German—had never known the man. Steve explained it. He had originally been put on to the problem of the squatters and Dorstman's parking garage project by his Dutch buddies, who had old friends among the squatters and who, through these old friends, had come to know all the people who had moved in on those shut-down Dorstman buildings. Piet Claes and the foreigners had been different.

"None of us knew any of the down-and-out unemployed," he said, "not until I got to know them through becoming involved in their problem with Dorstman."

"Piet, Sean, Whitey, and Kraky," I said. "They also became involved."

"They're not Steve," Julie said.

"What does *that* mean?"

I expected it would be the Europeans-and-Americans difference again, but this was something else. Steve's involvement was involvement with people. The others were by nature more aloof. Their involvement had been one of principle, involvement with a cause.

"It's the way they are," Steve said. "They don't really care about people as individuals. They just don't see men, because they have their sights fixed on mankind."

He didn't have to tell me any more. In one part of the world and another, I'd had some experience with terrorists. Steve had now given me a definitive description of their mental set.

"The guys who knew Groen," I said. "We should be talking to them. They might have some idea of any enemies he had."

"They'll be over at my place," Julie said. "They were going to wait for me there. I was coming back to tell them what was happening to Steve."

"Will they still be waiting?"

"They'll be waiting," Julie said. "By now they'll be going crazy."

"They don't care that much," Steve said.

"They do, Steve," Julie insisted. "I saw how they were, and you didn't. They love you like brothers."

"Even though they're European and Steve's not?" I asked.

I tossed that in because I thought it was time she pulled up her mental socks. All she did was pull gender on me.

"It's so complicated," she said. "No man could possibly understand."

Since, in any event, there was quick agreement that the brothers couldn't be kept waiting any longer, they came around to the garage with me to get Baby and I ran them around to Julie's place. They were all there and there wasn't much anyone could say until they had each of them had his turn at hugging Steve and pounding him on his back. Piet Claes did get to talk, at least enough to scold Steve for having gone around to the police station and to tell him that one of these days one or another of them was going to have to whip his britches.

By that time the lot of them were turning to Julie and hugging her. Instead of pounding her on the back, however, they were kissing her. They loved her, too, because she had freed Steve from durance vile.

By the time that simmered down, Julie and Steve made the mistake of explaining to them that it had been Erridge who had brought Van Mieris into the act and that it was there that the credit should lie. That made it my turn for taking the full round of huggings and back-slappings. I had the feeling that they might have been piling it on me in double measure since they couldn't get at Van Mieris.

Although it had seemed as though all that might have lasted forever, of course it didn't. They simmered down and the talk turned to the spy in their midst. Sean and Whitey were vocal and violent. The rat had to be unmasked and exterminated. Exterminated was the Frenchman's word. The Irishman was saying that he had to be executed. The ultimate savagery, however, was coming from Piet Claes. He was full of ideas of what must be done to the guy before they killed him. He was equally enchanted with the thought of cutting his tongue out and of castrating him. He was having difficulty choosing between the two, since the one would be symbolically appropriate and the other, I gathered, more fun.

Steve made a try at turning it off.

"It doesn't matter anymore," he said. "What matters is the guy who killed Groen. He also has to be one of us."

"Why one of us?" Sean asked.

"Who else knew we were hanging the effigies?"

"Someone came along after we hung them," Sean said. "He had a body to dispose of and he thought it was a great place to put it."

Whitey made his contribution of French logic. Since Dorstman had a spy, Dorstman had known about the effigies. Dorstman was Groen's enemy. So Q.E.D. He could have been giving us the proof to some simple problem in plane geometry. It was an opening and I took it.

"Dorstman had already done his worst on the poor guy," I said. "What about an enemy who felt or could feel that he still had a score to settle with Groen. Anybody know enough about him to have any ideas?"

Whitey wasn't ready to relinquish his proof. He argued that, since Groen had not been convicted of the charges Dorstman had laid against him, Dorstman could have felt that he still had a score to settle. I argued that it was logical but unreal.

Meanwhile the Dutch contingent had picked up on it. They were kicking it around among themselves, but that was in Dutch and I had to wait for a translation. Steve dismissed it.

"They have no ideas," he said.

Whitey jumped in to correct him. "That's not quite right," he said. "Jan is saying that Groen's worst enemy, even worse than Dorstman, was the bitch, his wife."

"I know what he's saying," Steve argued, "but you've got to be Jan even to think it. She's not in Amsterdam. She's nowhere even near. She left him even before his trial and she went home to Aachen." He turned to explain to me. "Groen had a German wife and no question that she's a bitch. The minute he was in trouble, she ran out on him, didn't stand by the guy even for a minute."

"I suppose nobody knows where in Aachen," I said.

Jan Maes knew. He came up with the information that she had a job selling in a cake shop and she lived next door to the shop. He knew this by accident. He had been there and had dropped in at the shop for a snack. The minute he had been in the place he had spotted her. It was understandable. If a woman was in a cake shop, it would have been inevitable that fat Jan would find her.

He knew the address, or at least he was able to describe the location of the shop. It was probably the only place in the whole city of Aachen that I was going to be able to find easily.

I had been through Aachen once, but that was long in the past. It was in the early years after the war and Aachen had then been a wasteland of shattered rubble with only a bit of its ancient center left standing. The biggest thing there, sticking up out of the wreckage, had been Charlemagne's Chapel. Jan was now telling me that the *Konditorei* was directly opposite Charlemagne's Chapel.

When that much had been translated for me, Julie broke in on it.

"The police will be talking to her," she said. "If she knows anything, they'll find out."

It was an opinion that won general agreement and the talk switched back to Dorstman's spy and the savageries that were to be inflicted on him. Steve and Julie, with an assist from me, worked at trying to tamp that down. It went on for far too long a time, but when everything had been repeated too many times over, people began yawning and the company started drifting away. I waited it out and finally I was left alone with Julie and Steve.

"You're going down to Aachen to see her?" Steve said.

"It's worth a try."

"I'm going with you."

"You can't."

"Who says I can't?"

"You'll say you can't as soon as you've thought about it even for a minute."

"What am I to think about?"

"Van Mieris. You can't go out of the country. That'll be playing Van Mieris dirty. You were released to him and he's trusting you. I'd say you can't even go out of Amsterdam."

"Not even to go and come right back?"

He knew I was right and he was trying to fight clear of the knowledge.

"Not even that," I said.

"What if I asked Van Mieris . . ."

"Don't put it on him," I said. "It's something you have to do for him. Suppose you do ask him. He's a kind-hearted and generous old man. He might say yes, and then, if you are picked up at the border, it will kick back at him. You can't do it to Van Mieris, not even if you would be doing it with his consent."

"Damn," Steve said.

Back at the hotel I asked for an early call and through what was left of the night I caught myself some sleep. When the call woke me, I had hardly begun to be slept out. I made a stab at getting up, but by the time my feet hit the floor I was thinking better of it. I didn't need such an early start. Aachen sits just across the border at the southern tip of Holland. The run down there was going to take me almost the full length of the country, but it is a small country. It was going to be something a little less than 150 miles, and for Baby that would be next to noth-

ing at all. There was no point in getting down there so
early that the bake shop wouldn't even be open.

There was another reason as well for going back to
sleep. I was going to visit the widow. I couldn't go empty-
handed. Since it would be hours before anything would
be open for my necessary shopping, I rang back down to
the desk and asked for another, later wake-up call. I had a
good sleep and woke before that second call came
through.

Not knowing which I would need to be, tough or
charming, I decided that the preparations I would have
to make should lie in the direction of charm. Toughness
would require no preparation. I gave careful attention to
my shave and serious study to what I was going to wear. I
worked hard that morning at making myself beautiful.
Surveying the result before I pulled out of the hotel room,
I even felt that I had not been unsuccessful.

I had a leisurely breakfast and did my shopping. It was
a big box of great Dutch chocolates, a fancy box or-
namented with enough yardage of blue satin ribbon
to have easily taken care of all the prize-giving at a
county fair. Ignorant of the lady's tastes and habits, I
went on to a liquor store, where I hedged my bet with a
bottle of good cognac. A little later, when I was already
on the road, I wondered whether it wouldn't have been
better if it had been Asbach Uralt, but booze is booze and
I let myself hope that she wouldn't be chauvinist about
her tipple.

It's a good road all the way down past Utrecht and
Eindhoven and then down in that little neck, where for a
brief space Holland holds Belgium and Germany apart, a
switch off the E9 to head east for the short run on the A3
over the border into Aachen.

It was late morning when I spotted the Konditorei sign and pulled into a parking spot near the bake shop. It was just the hour for the German custom of coffee and pastry that they call *Zweite Frühstück*—second breakfast.

I snagged a table and held my order down to coffee and the simplest of the many coffee cakes. The waitress tried to push one of the great monuments of heaped-up whipped cream. Though from the size and shape of her I knew that she was making her recommendations on more than hearsay, I insisted on being Spartan, but not to any extent that would knock off a chance of conversation.

Since my waitress and all the other women serving in the shop were too far along in years to have been Groen's wife, it was safe, when I asked for her, to take on the guise of an old friend come to see her.

"Frau Groen?" I asked.

"She doesn't work here anymore," my waitress said.

"She doesn't work anywhere anymore," another one volunteered.

"She's in mourning." A third took a kinder tone.

"I should have such mourning," my waitress said. "Money and her man. She cries like a cat in a cream jug."

"She just lost her man," I said.

"That one? How can you lose something you've already thrown away?"

I busied myself with my coffee and cake and let the waitresses carry on without me. It was a gossip exchange that developed into a bit of an argument. None of the old babes was saying the first good word for her.

Frau Groen was a slut. On that there was quick and easy consensus. The old biddies were differing only on the question of her husband's life insurance. One contingent argued that no man would continue his wife as beneficiary of his life insurance after she had heartlessly abandoned him. The other opinion was that Groen would have done just that. It was generally agreed that the man had been a *dreck*. The argument arose from differences in their beliefs of how a dreck would behave.

Literally translated, it is a bathroom word, but idiomatic German usage has laundered it to mean a softly ineffectual person. What I had learned about Groen back in Amsterdam fitted neatly with this estimate of the man, even though there it had been put more politely.

I finished my second breakfast, insisted that I couldn't manage even one of the less monumental edifices of whipped cream, and pulled out to move next door in search of Frau Groen's flat. The building was typical for Aachen. Risen from its wartime ashes, it is a city that was built quickly and with no thought for anything but meeting immediate practical need. It is a city of gray monotony, each structure identical with the next and all looking as gray and barren as had been the ashes.

There was nothing slummy about the building. Its halls and stairs were shiningly clean, freshly painted, and in excellent repair. In its institutional look it was depressing. It had the look of a model jail or a model asylum. In sharp contrast to the look of scrubbed cleanliness, however, the hall and the stairs stank. It was the smell of fish and not of fresh-caught fish but of dead fish that had been too long off the ice.

I climbed the stairs and found the door that had fixed to it the little card that said "Freya Groen." Right there the stink was at its strongest and ranged alongside the doorstep there was the obvious source of it, a discarded pound-size tin that had contained fresh caviar. The stench alone identified it but alongside lay verification—

the lid with its label. Less offensive but no less revealing were the other discards standing alongside Freya Groen's doorstep—three empty champagne bottles. They were Dom Perignon, no less. Dirk Groen's wake had been a wingding.

I rang the bell. I had my finger poised to ring a second time when I heard sounds of stirring inside and I held back on it. It was a few moments before she opened the door, and from the look of her she had needed those few moments for shoving her feet into a pair of mules that dripped festoons of grubby ostrich feathers and to wrap around her nakedness a thin silk robe also festooned with the grubby feathers.

Her hair had been elaborately done sometime in the recent past and the contrived structure had since been ravaged. Her face was puffy with sleep and, on an easy guess, with drink. Her mascara had run and her makeup had smeared, but past all that you could see that, pulled together, she could be quite a dish. As she stood in the doorway, she was in equal measure attractive and repulsive, like a George Grosz whore.

Wrinkling her nose, she had a few choice words for a slob of a janitor who hadn't yet removed the garbage. Simultaneously, however, she was taking quick note of the packages I was carrying. The candy box declared itself openly in all its beribboned flamboyance. My other package was suggestively bottle-shaped.

Without any question of who I was or what I wanted, she asked me in. Perhaps she found me so readily acceptable, or it may have been that the ready acceptance was for the burdens I carried. Inside I kicked the door shut behind me as I put the candy box into her hands and began unwrapping the cognac bottle.

"Frau Groen," I said. "I was sorry to hear about your husband."

"He brought it on himself," she said. "He brought everything on himself. He had a good job. He was doing well. Nobody asked him to be a thief."

I opened the bottle and I was looking around for a couple of clean glasses. She picked up a couple of used ones and, rubbing them inside and out with the hem of her robe, set them up for me to pour. I fished a stray bit of ostrich feather out of one of them and I poured. It was no time for being hobbled by hygiene.

"According to the verdict of the court," I said, "he wasn't a thief."

"That's all the court knows," she said, grabbing for her cognac.

"You know different?"

"I was his wife."

"Nobody can know better than a wife," I said. "I've been thinking you might know if he had any enemies."

"Who are you to be asking?"

I had to lie a little. I introduced myself and said something vague about having known her husband and liking him.

"I never saw you," she said.

"I didn't know Dirk until recently."

"You?"

She gave me an appraising look. It covered me from head to toe. She was making estimates of price for everything I had on me.

"I was going to give him a job," I lied.

She tossed off her cognac and shoved her glass out for more. I poured.

"Oh, that way," she said. "He went to live with scum.

You live with scum and you don't need enemies. You'll have friends who will murder you for a couple of *pfennig*."

We went on and on about pennies as the price of murder while she soaked up one great tot of the cognac after another. I was pacing myself on it and thinking that I should have gone for the whipped cream. It might have been a buffer against the alcohol. She seemed to be taking no notice of the fact that I wasn't going along with her drink for drink. If she was thinking about that at all, it would only have been a lush's greedy thought that it was leaving more for her.

Her flat was a one-roomer. She had taken the first cognac perched on the edge of her unmade bed. Relaxation came by not too slow stages and before long she was lying full length on the bed.

Meanwhile we were going round and round about enemies and scum. It was all variations on the one theme and it was going nowhere. Inevitably her eyelids started drooping. I kept it going until she was passed out.

Then I began searching the room.

CHAPTER 10

I had no definite idea of what I was looking for unless it was Groen's life-insurance policy. That had figured so heavily in the bake shop gossip that I was ready to consider it a factor that couldn't be ignored. Otherwise, I was thinking of letters. I came on the insurance policy almost at once.

It was out in plain sight, lying on her bedside table. Under it was a canceled check dated only a month earlier. It was drawn to the insurance company and signed by her. She had been keeping up the premium payments. Though the premium was small, I found it interesting. I checked the policy. It was for guilder that would translate to about $50,000 straight life. The issue date was far enough back to indicate that Groen had taken the insurance when he was still very young. Start one early enough for the actuarial calculations to give you a long remaining life expectancy, and you get it cheap.

I put the policy and the check back on the table and looked around for anything else that might be out in plain sight. The room was a littered mess, but I could see nothing in the litter to indicate anything but that Frau Freya Groen was a slob.

I started checking drawers and cupboards. Both were tangles of things that had been stuffed away when they should either have been laundered or sent out for cleaning. The only things that looked clean and fresh were a couple of uniforms such as I had seen next door on her former colleagues of the bake shop.

So far as was possible, in the disordered messes of the drawers, I was trying to go through everything systematically. I was finding no letters and nothing else that could possibly have been of any significance. I was just delving through more than anyone could have wanted of Frau Freya Groen's unwashed laundry.

It was in a bottom drawer and at the very bottom of it, too, that my hand touched something solid. As I took a grip on it, I knew just by feel what it was. Smooth metal, flat glass, twisted wire—my fingers were telling me picture frame. I was thinking it would be a picture of her late husband, but I pulled it out from under all the tangled junk that had been piled in on top of it. It had been in the drawer face down and I brought it out face down. I was straightening up from bending to the drawer and about to turn the picture over to look at it when I felt the unmistakable jab hit my spine.

Even before she spoke, I knew it for what it was—the muzzle of a gun poked into me at a spot where a shot, if it wouldn't be sudden death, would at least be a lifetime paralysis.

"Drop that," she said. "If you even begin to turn it over, I'll shoot."

When I had first felt that gun muzzle poke into me, I'd thought I could handle it. I thought she was making the mistake often made by people with a knowledge of guns that is only an insufficient knowledge. Jam a gun tight against a man's body and you're in a position where you can't miss. What's wrong with it is that you are also in a position where, if he has the guts and he knows his stuff, you're not ever going to get to shoot him.

A swinging arm moves faster than any finger, and a body can swing aside faster than a trigger can be squeezed or even jerked. It was good thinking, but Frau Groen had sufficient knowledge. She didn't leave her gun muzzle tight against my back for any longer than was needed to let me know it was there. She immediately backed off with it, not far but just far enough to be out of my reach with the revolver leveled dead on me.

I turned to face her and the gun. Her hand was shaking, but I could see that it wasn't from nerves. It was just from drink. Anyhow, it wasn't shaking so much that at the short range her shot wouldn't be going into my belly. An inch or two this way or that wasn't going to make much difference when I would be taking it in the belly. That area is too tightly packed with indispensable organs to be laughed off.

My yellow streak is no broader than the next man's, but only a fool argues with a gun. I took her at her word and dropped the frame without ever looking at the picture. I didn't have to look at it. I had learned enough. The police back in Amsterdam could take this thing from there.

"You passed out on me," I said. "I had nothing to do and nobody to talk to. I just got bored."

Reaching out, she closed her free hand over the telephone.

"Get out," she said, "or do I call the police?"

"We were having fun," I said.

"Until you got bored. Now *I* am bored. Get out and never come back."

I moved toward the door.

"*Auf wiedersehen, Liebchen,*" I said.

"Get out."

I left and shut the door behind me. Outside it was dusk. The street lights had come on. There would be nothing more for me in Aachen. It was time I was hitting the road back to Amsterdam. As I was climbing into the Porsche, I looked back. The curtain at her window was stirring. She was up there watching me take off.

I was going to take the highway for the quickest run back to Amsterdam, and there I was going to head straight for the police station and my inquisitor. I had disappointed the man. I'd had no answers for him. Now I was going to make it up to him.

If she was at all smart, of course, she had already had the picture I didn't see out of the frame and she had flushed it down the john. It would be enough, however, that there had been a picture and that there was the insurance policy on which the estranged wife had been keeping up the premiums. I had a lead to give my inquisitor man and I had no doubt of its being a big fat lead.

Dark overtook me before I was off the A3 and, zipping along in Baby up the E9, I began building a headache. I made the mistake of thinking I could handle it with Maigret's remedy and I stopped for a beer. Maybe I'm not the man Maigret was, or maybe it was just not that kind of a headache. Mine grew up into the blinding range and I had stomach sensations along with it. This head of mine wasn't yammering for a beer. It was telling me that my stomach was yammering for food. I had eaten nothing since that *Zweite Frühstück* and that hadn't been feeding as much as it had been research. I couldn't remember that Maigret had ever let himself miss a meal.

I tried to handle it by promising myself the biggest of all dinners once I had reached Amsterdam and had been to the police. It was the worst possible approach. Thinking about food only made things worse.

The sight of a roadside restaurant broke me down completely. I had pushed myself beyond my limit. I pulled up and went in. I ordered the biggest steak they could come up with. The accompaniment to that big a steak was something that fell not much short of a bushel of fries. Even the heavy-feeding Dutch showed some astonishment as they watched me wolf all that down; but I was shameless and, in any case, it was awed and admiring astonishment.

I came out of the restaurant a new man, slightly dopey with the sudden swing from starvation to surfeit, but well pleased with myself and the world. I had been thinking about the picture it was death to see, and the only thought I had been able to come up with was Fredrik Dorstman. That the old goat should have gone for the younger man's luscious wife was conceivable. That he should have conspired with her to murder the man for his insurance was not.

To a Fredrik Dorstman fifty grand would be too piddling a sum. I was ready to believe the man was greedy, but his would be a greed that would reach for millions. I was thinking, therefore, that the insurance money would be the widow's delight, and Dorstman's the widow herself.

As I headed for the parking lot, all such speculations fell away. Parked alongside the Porsche there was a small panel truck. Small panel trucks are not rare objects and, even as I was telling myself that there was no reason to think that this one would be Steve Dale's, I was also telling myself that there was no reason to think it was not.

His was just like it, and the one I had seen by the foot-bridge across the canal had also been just like it.

I wasn't permitting myself to forget that when I had seen such a truck by the footbridge there had been that quick hit on the head to wipe out all sight of it. I had no wish to soak up another knockout clunk. There is no time when I would welcome one of those, but this time I had to recognize that it might very likely be a thing of larger dimensions. I was telling myself that it wouldn't be alarmist to think of it even in terms of lethal dimensions.

When I had left Frau Freya Groen, she'd had only one hand filled with gun. The other had been wrapped around the telephone. She had threatened using it to call the police. Once my retreat had relieved her of any such necessity, could she not have used it to ring through to Amsterdam to report on my visit?

This little truck could have been riding the highway in the hope of catching up with me before I could be back in Amsterdam. It wouldn't have been too unpromising a venture. It could have been assumed that I would have been taking the shortest and fastest route and, as my police inquisitor had remarked, Baby is a spectacular. She is all too easy to spot.

It could be a menace, but it could also be an opportunity. It took not even a moment of inner struggle to bring me down on the side of opportunity. Assuming the guise of a man who is heedless of everything but his love for his wheels, I moved in on the Porsche and bent over to inspect Baby's tires. Suckering myself into taking a quick hit? I was working at making it look that way, but I was tensed and waiting.

With nightfall a chill wind had come up. It was at my back and, bent over as I was to inspect Baby's tires, I could feel it on the backs of my calves and thighs and on my butt. Then I wasn't feeling it. It could have been that the wind had died down, but winds don't ordinarily die such sudden deaths. It is more in the nature of a wind to dwindle.

In any case it wasn't going to matter. If I did the fast pivot and grab and I grabbed nothing but the empty air, it would be nothing lost. I moved. I moved fast and I put all my weight into it. I didn't come up with empty air. My shoulder made contact even as a mean-sounding swish whizzed past my ear. The contact was violent and it caught the man just back of the knee. It was a clip. There was nothing else you could have called it. If there had been a referee on the ground, I would have been penalized fifteen yards, but we weren't boys at play. We were men at work, and I was appointing myself referee.

I had my arms wrapped around his legs. I brought him down and I sat on him. It was too dark to see who it was, but identification could wait. It was enough for me that I had the man I wanted, whoever he might be. He struggled, but I'd brought him down with enough force to take most of the fight out of him. I had little trouble handling him. I took off his belt and used it to secure his hands behind his back. My own belt served for lashing his ankles together. I had no worry about losing my slacks. The way Caraceni builds them, they stay up on their own. I couldn't be concerned about the possibility that he might lose his. That would have been the least of what he stood to lose.

I jerked the man to his feet and, keeping a tight grip on him with one arm, I reached over and switched on Baby's lights. She has a pivoting spot. I turned it to shine the beam on him. The beam fell on the ground and there was a moment before I had the light tipped up to show me his face.

On the ground by our feet lay a hockey stick. It wasn't one of the light jobs little kids play with. This one was man-sized. You've seen them on the ice if you've ever watched the pros. You may even have seen them crack skulls. That was the thing that had swished past my ear when I had been doing my pivot out from under it.

As I was tipping the light up, the beam hit his right hand. I suppose he was too groggy to know it, but he still had clutched in that hand a loop of wire. If it wasn't the one that had been used to garrote Groen, it would only be that he kept a supply of them against any time of need. I took note of those items in passing, but I wasn't lingering over them. I brought the light up onto his face. I had been certain that it would be a face I knew and I wasn't disappointed. It was Piet Claes.

A sane man at that point would have dragged him into the restaurant and called the police. Utrecht could have gotten on to Amsterdam, and I would have had him off my hands. I didn't want the rat off my hands, not that quickly. I was feeling too savage for doing it the easy way.

I dumped him into the back of the Porsche and, kneeling on him there, I took his tie off. The sweat shirt and jeans evidently were only one-of-the-boys uniform. On his own, he wore a tie. I liked that. It saved me using my own and that I would have hated, since I was wearing one of Atkinson's Irish poplins for which I have a great fondness and my schedule offered no quick opportunity to be in Dublin to pick up a replacement.

His tie did very well. I used it to fasten the belt around his wrists to the belt around his ankles. Trussed up that way, he was going to be no worry to me during the short remaining run up to Amsterdam.

I picked up the hockey stick and tossed it in on top of him. I took great care in the way I handled it. I wasn't putting any fingerprints of mine on any part of it a man could grasp if he was going to swing it. I pulled Baby out to the E9 and induced her to give her speedy all.

For a while he was perfectly still. Then he took to thrashing about. That didn't trouble me. The way I had him secured, he could do himself no good. If he chose to beat up on himself, that suited me fine. It compensated me somewhat for my self-restraint. I could have much enjoyed beating up on him myself.

We were off the highway and into the city streets before he spoke, or maybe he had spoken before that, but the way we'd been making time on the E9, the wind of our going would have blown his words away from me. The city traffic forced me to slow down some. Then I could hear.

"You'll never get away with this," he was saying. "It's kidnaping."

"You're no kid," I said, "and what makes you think I'm napping?"

"If you think this is a joke," he said.

"I don't laugh at murder."

"You're going to kill me?"

"I'd like to, but I can't," I said. "It's the disadvantage of being civilized. It deprives a man of all kinds of savage fun. I'm taking you to the police."

"You didn't in Utrecht. What are you doing? What do you want?"

"The Amsterdam police asked for my cooperation," I

said, "and I promised it. I'm keeping my promise. I'm cooperating."

"You'll see what they think of kidnaping."

"I know what they think of murder."

"I didn't," he said.

"You'll be taking that up with them."

He kept yammering about kidnaping. He tried to tell me that I was making the mistake of thinking he was Dorstman's spy and that I was taking him to the gang for gang punishment.

"I couldn't do that," I said. "They might remember your recommendations. You know. Flip a coin. Heads your tongue, tails your balls."

He tried to tell me I was wrong. They knew him and they didn't know me. They would never believe me. They were going to get on to the game I was playing and they would deal with me. He even came up with a translation of what he said was an old Dutch proverb:

"People with butter on their hands shouldn't go out in the sun."

We say "glass houses." They say "butter on their hands." I just let him talk. I couldn't think of any more one-liners, and the ones I'd handed him had been wasted.

I pulled up at the police station and I handed him over along with the hockey stick and the loop of wire. That was lying on the floor of the car. Sometime during the ride to Amsterdam he'd had wit enough to drop it out of his hand. He probably would have liked to have tossed it out of the car, but the way I had him tied up had given him no tossing room. It isn't likely that he would have been given pause by the fact that Dutch laws are rough on littering.

He yelled kidnaping and, of course, there was nowhere

he could go with that, since it's the odd kidnaper who pulls off his caper with no purpose but to hand his victim over to the cops. I told my story and, when it had been typed up, I signed it. I was heartily thanked and I promised that, if needed, I would make myself available to testify.

As soon as I was clear of the police station, I whipped around to Julie's place. There was nobody home. I tried the studio and found her there with Steve. They were alone. They had some trouble with believing Claes could be a murderer. The role of spy struck them as being an easier fit.

Steve gave little time to discussing it. He was quickly up and away to find the other guys and to tell them the news. That, he said, was the first order of business. They had to be told before one of them would fasten on another and somebody would be bumped off. They were all of them out on the spy hunt.

Julie went with him but, before we parted, she kissed me.

The police took it from there. Nobody ever saw the picture. They did come up with the frame, but it was without evidential value since it contained only a publicity shot of Elvis Presley. That was to have been expected. Piet Claes had been flushed down the john.

It didn't matter. There were the waitresses down in the Konditorei and they had seen Freya Groen's lover. With unshakable unanimity they picked Piet Claes out of a lineup. With that much for a start, the police knew which way to go. They had a thread and it took them all the way.

Piet Claes had been the embezzler and he had framed Dirk Groen for it. The frame hadn't been a complete success since Groen had been acquitted, but insofar as it had ruined Groen, it had been almost good enough. Almost, however, is less than perfect. Groen had been on the loose and he had been working at clearing himself in the hope of making it possible for him to reenter the job market.

He had come up with some evidence that was going to lead him to the truth, and Claes had slammed the door on that by knocking the poor guy off. Since Claes had not been part of the effigy-hanging party, he'd thought it a brilliant idea to insert Groen's body in the row of hanged effigies and to dispose of the displaced effigy in a way he'd hoped would have the police looking at me and at the hangmen.

He had known, as the whole bunch of them did, that it was Julie's assignment to keep me immobilized during that evening when they would be doing the hanging. When Steve came home from hanging the effigies, as usual he left his truck parked in the street. Claes took it, loaded Groen's body in it, and went out to the demolition site to make the switch. With the removed effigy now in the truck, he had returned to wait parked in Julie's street.

He had seen me bring her home from our evening on the town and, when I left her, he followed me. Just what he had in mind as a spot to dump the effigy where the police would inevitably link it to me it is impossible to know.

It's my guess that he had been hoping I would leave the Porsche in street parking. In that event he could have dumped the dummy into Baby. Since I garaged her, that was no good. After that, he was stuck with creeping after me in the truck while I was going back to the hotel on foot.

As soon as he saw that the direction I was taking meant

that I would be crossing the canal by the footbridge, he had known that he would have to act then or else lose me. He couldn't take the truck over the footbridge.

He pulled up there and conked me on the head. He had time for only the hastiest and most unconvincing job of robbing me, since he also had to rid himself of the effigy before I would come around. He did as much as the time allowed and he took off.

Julie and Steve got married. Van Mieris was unconscionably slow about getting our contract drawn up for the signing. He has never admitted that he dragged his feet on it because he was determined to keep me in Amsterdam for the wedding. He insisted on their being married in his house and he put on the wedding reception that must be one of the great parties of all time.

I gave the bride away, a gesture of the most uncharacteristic generosity.

Since Van Mieris made some additions of his own to the guest list furnished to him by Julie and Steve, Fredrik Dorstman was among the invited guests. Van Mieris' recent additions to his art collection—the poster and the plaster head—were prominently displayed. That they were given so conspicuous a position among Jan's Mondriaans and Van Goghs may have been in the bridegroom's honor. I think not. Dorstman managed to laugh, but he didn't stay long at the party.

I got to kiss the bride, but when you are standing in line for it along with all the other wedding guests, it's not the same.

About the Author

Aaron Marc Stein graduated from Princeton with a degree in classics and archaeology. His first novel was published on the recommendation of Theodore Dreiser. He has published nearly one hundred novels in the Crime Club, a body of work for which he has received the Mystery Writers of America's Grand Master Award. Mr. Stein has chronicled the adventures of Matt Erridge in such previous novels as *A Body for a Buddy, A Nose for It, The Cheating Butcher,* and *Chill Factor*. He lives in New York City.